The Price of Crabs

A Novel

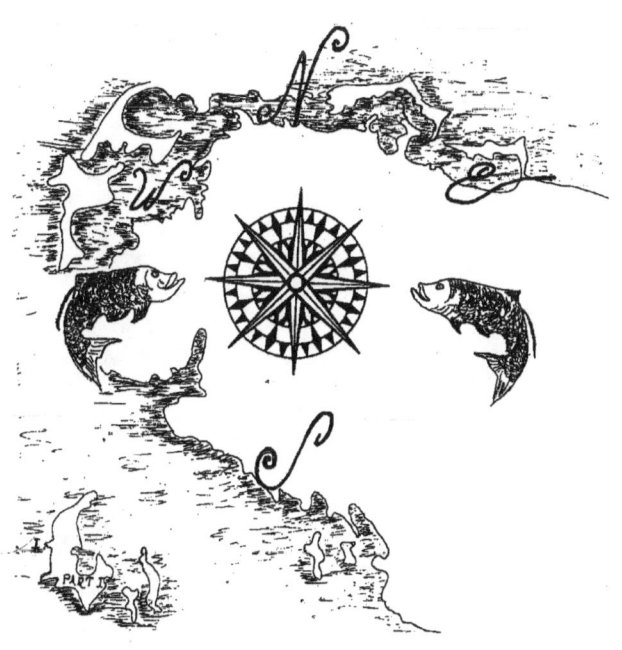

CAROLYN SIEMON SCHÖNER

Also by Carolyn Siemon Schöner

When The Muse Whispers

Watch for her new book

The Wounded Souls

This is a work of fiction. Names, characters, businesses, places, events and incidents are either the products of the author's imagination or used in a fictitious manner. Any resemblance to actual persons, living or dead, or actual events is purely coincidental.

In 1989 The State of Florida put a ban on all tortoise racing especially gopher turtles. The Gopher Tortoise population has dropped significantly since 1960's and they are presently on the endangered list. I am not sure the turtle races contributed to the loss of the tortoise as much as the disappearance of their natural habitant.

Revised - Second Addition
©Copyright 2017 by Carolyn Siemon Schöner
All rights reserved
Printed in the United States of America
Siemon Schöner Publishing
Englewood, FL 34223
ISBN - 978-0-578-19107-2

Interior art by Carolyn Siemon Schöner

For Carl and Carmela

Praise for The Price of Crabs

Carolyn is a fine storyteller, weaving a tale that vividly depicts scenes, fascinating characters, and events from the Florida of my youth. This colorful glimpse into a pristine paradise and simple life, which was once Englewood, brings a tear to the eye of those who will forever miss the beauty of nature teeming with life, and grieve the loss of all things wild.

Janice Williams

I enjoyed the nostalgic theme of your story; it has a rhythm like the clackety-clack of the old wooden bridges, especially the casualness and relaxed atmosphere of old Florida. What is the end result of the love story between Isabella and Jerry?

Betty Dailey-Nugent
Southwest Historic Organization Resources and Education (SHORE), Friend of Sarasota County History Society

An engaging read! Carolyn Schöner takes us on a journey back in time prior to the development of Florida's west coast with a cast of colorful characters, a dash of history, mystery and a profound title that will leave you pondering The Price of Crabs.

Karl Simmons
Coarsegold, CA

The Price of Crabs is an intimate glance through rosy shades of the charming world that was old Florida; Schöner seems to have bottled up the magic of both the people and the place, delivering from pen to paper in a way that can only be described as pure nostalgia.

P. S. Nichols

It's a rollicking good read! Carolyn introduces you to a cast of zany characters and brings to life old Englewood. So crack the covers of this book and settle down for a fascinating trip to a time past.

Joan Anacreon-Karatzas

Forward

Many Baby Boomers came of age as Rachel Carson galvanized the environmentalist movement with "Silent Spring." Since then, we've all come to know the peril posed by human failure to appreciate and sustain the natural life that is our birthright. Through the years, the evidence of environmental damage has grown as clear and present as global warming.

Yet champions of the environment are often drowned out by the almighty dollar or the gloominess of their message.

Carolyn Siemon Schöner, in "The Price of Crabs," has managed to convey the anger and pain of environmental desecration in a voice that sounds like music and reads like poetry. The grace and humor with which she tells her story will make even the most skeptical reader reconsider the responsibility we all have to respect our birthright from Mother Nature.

Schöner understands that the little fibers of cause and effect, when woven well, create a fabric that's enduring. Consider, from the book, the three scenes on the Indian mound.

The characters' divergent reactions shape a satisfying experience. One pontificates, one muses, and one reaps the fruit of preservation in an ironic fashion.

There are truths, and then there are well-told truths. "The Price of Crabs" tells the truth well.

James Abraham
Book-broker Publishers of Florida

Contents

Boca Grande - 1989

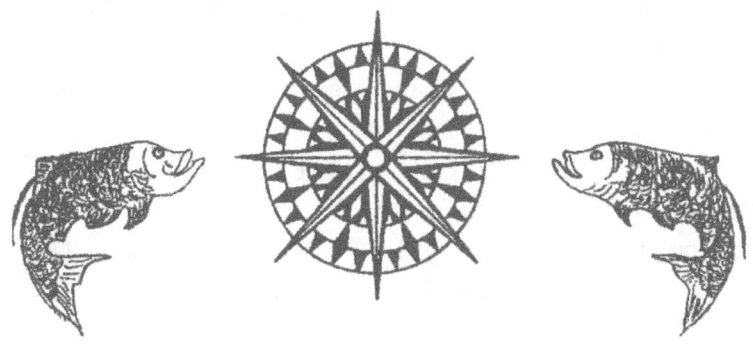

The Price of Crabs

*K*ate wiped the condensation off the ice cream coolers for the umpteenth time as she heard the clack-clack of the Turtle Creek Bridge. She waited. Usually it took forty-five seconds to reach the Shell Creek Bridge. She crossed the ice cream shop and stood in front of the window. "Another hot day." Already, at ten a.m., the temperature had soared into the nineties', with the humidity it seemed like a hundred and ten degrees. Heat wafted off the payment in lazy clouds of vapor.

A tourist stopped and photographed Bob's Bait

House across the road. It was an old clapboard house with peeling, gray paint. Colored floats caught in fishnets decorated the front walls; a mullet boat lay on its side. The owner abandoned the boat several years ago. Bob rescued it and then painted it bright colors, placed two crab traps inside and added a rusted anchor. Instant Florida landmark.

Bob was more closed than open. Today a sign hung on the door. "GONE FISHING" was enameled in neon yellow to match the floats caught in the netting. The tourist took few photographs, then got back in the car and headed north across the Shell Creek Bridge. The sound of dry wood creaking under the weight of the car punctuated the stillness.

I love these wooden bridges, Kate thought. She told time by their rhythmic clackety-clack. The sound lulled her to sleep at night and the clackety-clack; clackety-clack of the fishermen crossing early in the morning on their way to the Landing was her alarm clock.

She made the fishermen coffee early in the morning, sometimes they twisted her arm enough that she fried them an egg or two along with toast and bacon. They never paid in cash for the breakfasts, but rewarded Kate with fresh fish, smoked mullet, an occasional side of deer meat, and sometimes a wild boar for barbecuing.

To the north of the small island surrounded by mangroves was the Landing, where the mullet fishermen keep their boats on Shell Creek. South of her ice cream shop was a row of old, abandoned clapboard shacks with bougainvillea growing through the windows and untrimmed orange trees covering the front yards. The only inhabitants were a few stray dogs who lazily lifted their heads at the passing cars. The shacks were left over from the days of the turpentine camps that once lined the river. Back then, the few colored people who lived there worked for the wealthy resident of the key. Kate saw mystic romance in the abandoned cabins.

The clapboards were weathered gray; an occasional dwelling had hanging shutters with peeled aqua blue paint. Large traveler palms, royal poinsettias, and wild jasmine vines dwarfed many. During winter, seasonal artists would show up and maybe two or three would set up along the road and paint furiously, ignoring the sweat, bugs, and mosquitoes.

All that has changed and the only remnants are shacks along Turtle Creek. Both creeks empty into the bay, which flows two miles to the Gulf of Mexico.

It seems like a strange place to sell ice cream, on a small island at the edge of nowhere. But Kate had the only ice cream shop in a stretch of ninety-six miles--the only air-conditioned ice cream shop. Besides ice cream, she sold stick candy, a few gifts, cheap greeting cards, souvenirs made from shells, and small household items. Her store was the go-to place for flypaper, fly swatters, hand fans, bug spray, dustpans, clothespins, and assorted sundries. She also kept special books, crayons, and pencils for children. She had a couple of old wooden desks with wrought-iron rungs and inkwells. In the middle of a Florida key, Kate's shop had New England flair, with its paneled wall, antiques, and old wire ice cream table and chairs.

A pickup truck's gears resounded as it crossed the Turtle Creek Bridge; it slowed down and pulled into the yard. Good, customers, Kate thought, ceasing her endless wiping of condensation from the fogged-up windows. She recognized the truck; it belonged to the Crab Lady. The three of them, a woman and two males, lumbered into the store kind of slow and deliberate, the way they always moved.

Kate, an outsider who had only been on the island two years, wondered about the trio. Gossip had it that she left an elegant life style to be with him and raise his son. She knew they lived in the Shell Creek fish lagoon in a shack on stilts, with no electricity or running water.

The Crab Lady was tall, six feet if not more. She was a big woman, not fat but big-boned. She kept her hair pulled back and tied in a knot, like a New York society matron. Her skin was like cracked leather from years in the sun. She had beautiful white teeth, straight and almost florescent against her swarthy skin. She had a straight nose and clear blue eyes. She stood aloof and stiff, as if a board ran up her back. She wore oversized overalls, yellow fishing boots and, despite the heat, a faded flannel shirt. Besides her tattered clothing, an air of good breeding marked her.

Everything else was askew. Her companion was short, skinny, toothless, dirty, smelly, and small. He made a beeline for the ice cream coolers, without a word of greeting for Kate. His red eyes darted from one flavor to the next. His small red tongue rimmed his lips in anticipation. He argued with himself, his animal-like noises of deliberation echoing in the small store, as he debated butter pecan, no, chocolate chip, no, rocky road, no, almond fudge, no, pistachio, no, New York cherry, no. He rubbed his hands up and down his pants as he walked back and forth, trying to make up his mind. However, invariably, he settled for vanilla, as he has done a thousand times before.

"In, in, a, a, dish, no cone for me."

Kate served him an extra-large scoop.

"Hot fudge sauce, maybe a little whipping cream?" Kate asked.

"Hot fudge."

Kate handed him the dish of ice cream. He smiled a wonderful toothless smile exposing cherry-red gums. When he reached for the dish, she noticed his hands were covered with raw sores from pulling crab traps all day. Kate averted her eyes.

He always had his son with him. The son knew exactly what he wanted.

"Strawberry in a sugar cone," he said with a tentative look at his dad. "It's okay, right?"

"Yep," the man said, as he spooned the stray rivulets of ice cream streaming from the mound in the dish.

Kate rolled the ice cream round and round to make a large scoop and placed it high on the boy's sugar cone. She gave him a large smile. Kate always was awkward around the boy and the man. The boy always drooled saliva from the corners of his mouth.

The Crab Lady ordered a butter pecan cone with a

crisp New England accent, paid, and joined the rest of her family at one of the wire tables.

Kate watched them as she wiped the accumulating moisture on the ice cream cooler's glass front. Why was she here? What's wrong with this picture? A tall, elegant lady with a Boston accent, her hair tied severely in a knot at the nape of her neck, sharing ice cream with a soiled, crusty little man with dirt caked under his fingernails, a few hairs matted to his head, no teeth to chew with, smelling of fish three days old, and with a retarded son.

She must love him, Kate thought. But no, there had to be another reason, maybe he had money hidden at the bottom of the sea in one of his crab traps. At night, does he take a bath, put in his false teeth, don a suit, splash on Brute and turn into a prince? He kissing her, she kisses him. Kate tried to imagine them making love, she sucking on his manhood and he kissing her—

"May I have a glass of water?" the Crab Lady asks, shaking Kate from her reverie.

"Of course," Kate said. Was she reading my mind? She began to slap herself mentally for her evil thoughts as she served the three of them.

Who am I to judge? Kate thought as she returned to the endless task of wiping condensation. After all, my life is measured by the beat of the clackety-clack clamor of folks crossing the bridges to this godforsaken island.

Leave, she thought. Easy enough, just lock the door, walk across the Shell Creek Bridge, and never look back. Why did I move here? Because of the tranquility, the beauty, and because I can be at Stump Pass and look in both directions and not see another soul; that is why I am here. Because I can lie on the beach and listen to wind blow through the Australian Pines, because I can take my boat out into the Gulf twenty-five miles, still see bottom, and watch the fish swim under and around the boat. Mostly because I like to fish and the Gulf waters are crisp, clear, and full of sea life. I guess that is why I live between two bridges. Then the clackety-clack starts, my curiosity peeks and a new adventure begins. Back to work, she thought—and act like you have some sense.

"Here is a new book," she said, offering a book of colorful pictures to the son.

She was struck by the vacant look in his eyes. His father patted the top of his head and began to read aloud. His voice was amazing, like that of a thespian. Kate stopped wiping the coolers and listened. My shop is a stage, she thought, marking the man's measured speech and animated gestures. The Crab Lady took a paper napkin and wiped a silvery line of drool from the corner of the boy's mouth. Kate lowered her eyes in homage.

Clackety-clack, Clackety-clack

Two vehicles crossed the Shell Creek Bridge heading south. Kate listened for a few minutes and realized she had some new customers. Four men got out of their cars and walked into the Ice Cream Shoppe.

The spell was broken. Kate got an empty feeling in the pit of her stomach. The father put down the book. The boy laid his head upon the cover and appeared to go asleep.

The four men looked like clones. They all had the

same khaki cotton trousers, boat shoes, and cotton knit shirt, except that's where the discerning eye could spot the differences. One had a green shirt with an alligator embroidered on his left breast, one had a blue shirt with a horse sewn on his left breast, and the third one a yellow shirt with a penguin. The forth guy clearly had the money. He wore a white cotton shirt with the sleeves rolled up and what Kate guessed was his initials embroidered on his shirt. The garment had no pocket, which meant that it was custom made.

"Do you know where we can find the Crab Lady?" he asked.

Kate nodded, but before she can answer the Crab Lady spoke.

"Yes."

"We need some crabs for tarpon fishing."

Every year at this time the island got a parade of snowbirds seeking the "Sport of Kings." At the turn of the century tarpon fishing was truly that, as wealthy sportsmen invoked so many stipulations that only they could afford the sport. They had regulations on the type of rod, type of reel, weight of the line, and the size of boat. Now, with the arrival of the nouveau riche, the rules have changed and anyone can fish in a tarpon tournament. Kate recently saw a man in a canoe fishing with a cane pole.

"How may do you want?" she asked.

"At least a dozen," Mr. Alligator-logo said.

The temptation was so great Kate couldn't resist. "Is the dozen just for you or do you plan on sharing?" she asked.

The Crab Lady came to his rescue.

"I think for the four of you gentlemen, at least six dozen per tide should be plenty."

Mr. Penguin spoke up.

"Six dozen? Are they alive? How much a dozen?

"To answer your questions, yes, they are alive and will stay alive as long as you don't remove their pinchers," the Crab Lady said. "Six dozen for four men fishing is not a lot."

Mr. Horse just neighed something about taking off pinchers.

"I'll take them off the first dozen" the Crab Lady said, "and your guide will probably remove them as needed from the others."

Not only were the guys clones but they also were clowns. Not only did they dress alike, but they also looked alike, with scrubbed, tanned faces, capped teeth, and gold watches.

"Are your crabs small?" Mr. Alligator asked.

"Microscopically so" Kate said.

Mr. Alligator shot her a look. Kate just shrugged her shoulders. She smiled as she anticipated repeating, "Are your crabs small?" to her mullet fishing customers. It would be worth a few laughs over coffee.

Mr. Alligator asked again. "How much for a dozen crab?"

"Seven dollars."

"You're kidding. Seven dollars is too much, especially if we have to remove the pinchers."

"Alligator mouth and canary asshole," Kate blurted out.

The leader of the pack, turned and stared hard at Kate. Then he turned back to the Crab Lady.

"I am very curious," he said. "How do you remove the pinchers?"

"They have an elbow joint," she said. "You take your fishing pliers and apply pressure at the joint. The crab will voluntarily shed its pincher. Your hooks should be sharp. About half an inch from the point on the crab shell, you take the point of your hook and twist back and forth until that makes a hole. Then set the hook in place."

She kept their attention while she told of spring tides, swift flowing waters and how the tarpon love crabs. She told them where in the pass to fish and what guide was better than the next, then wound up her spiel by repeating, "The price for crabs is seven dollars a dozen."

Mr. Alligator darted a look at Kate, and again asked.

"Are your crabs small?"

"The crabs are the size of a silver dollar, thus called dollar crabs."

"Your price is too high."

Kate stopped cleaning the coolers for the sixtieth time that afternoon, and scrutinized the clone with the capped teeth and gold watch.

"What kind of rod and reel do you have?" she asked. "One of those new ones with the roller guides?"

"Why yes I do, I have a Penn International No. 30," he bragged. "I fish with a stout pole and fifty-pound braided Dacron line."

"Then it seems to me you can afford the price of the crabs," Kate snapped.

The gentleman in the white shirt made the decision.

"We'll take six dozen, and I want to watch you take the pinchers off."

He paid for six dozen and made arrangements to pick up the crabs in twenty minutes. The Crab Lady gave them directions. Negotiations over, she and her family left.

"How is the ice cream?" the lead gentleman asked.

"Wonderful."

"I'll have a strawberry sundae, whipped cream, nuts, and a cherry. How about the rest of you guys? I'm buying."

Alligator mouth proclaimed. "While you are eating your ice cream, we're going out to have a smoke."

"Kathryn Callahan," I'm Ed Harris, you are one of my best customers.

Kate's mouth dropped. "What?"

"I am CEO of American Food, Inc., you buy your ice cream from us."

"What are you doing here?"

"Well, when you contacted our sales department to purchase ice cream, that caused a logistic problem for us."

"What kind of topping do you want on your sundae?" Kate interrupted.

"If you don't mind I like hot fudge."

"Just how did I create a logistic problem?"

"First, we do not deliver this far south. There is a distribution center in Tampa. Our product line is extensive and most of the food manufacturers are north. Columbus, Ohio is our corporate office. We are heavy in dairy, milk, cheese, butter, yogurt, and ice cream. We are also in dry goods and frozen foods. To deliver your ice cream we need refrigeration and to send a truck down from Tampa is not cost effective." Ed stoped talking and started eating his sundae. "Mmmmm-mmm, it's good."

Kate was leaning on the cooler listening to his speech, wondering why this company went with her request; she did not know the answer was forth coming.

"Our demographics' department looked into this location and did a quick study. Southwest Florida is on the verge of expansion and development, there are shopping centers on the drawing boards, schools, expanded healthcare facilities, and the land developers are buying up land. Large grocery chains are planning to expand down here, from Bradenton to Naples. I made the decision to supply you, you were our first customer."

"You made the right decision." An over whelmed Kate responded.

"And this way I can tarpon fish and write off my trip."

Kate laughed, "Smart Analyses."

Ed placed his empty dish on the cooler and turned to leave; when he reached the door he turned and faced Kate.

"Kathryn, if I can shake these guys off for an afternoon would you like to have lunch?"

"I would be delighted."

Clackety-clack, clackety-clack

Ed and his companions crossed the Turtle Creek Bridge, on their way to the home of the Crab Lady, to buy and watch her prepare the crabs for tarpon fishing.

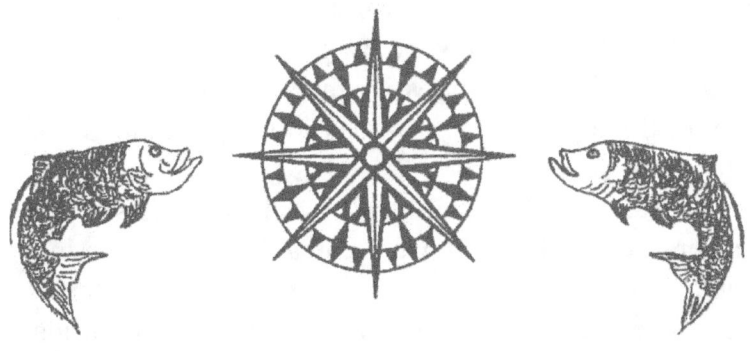

Tanqueray, Virgins, Pins, and Other Things

on Buyers stood naked in front of his plate glass window. Beads of water clung to his body from the steaming shower he had just taken. He watched the heavy nimbus clouds, their bellies full of snow, work their way across Lake Michigan on the wings of the northeast winds from Canada. He watched the whitecaps form on this bitter-cold day. The chill permeated through the Thermopane glass; his breath left a small circle of steam on the window. He wiped the condensation with his finger, but it came back quickly. The window rattled with the gusts of wind. He felt the cold through his whole body. His penis shriveled and he shivered yet he made no effort to leave his post.

The cold gnawed at him. Buyers could not shake the feelings of despair, of loneliness, and of worthlessness. He had been haunted by restlessness ever since his return from Florida. He knew he was successful. Everyone thought of him as a progressive thinker, a man's man. He had all the toys worthy of a man in his position, yet he felt empty.

It was Isabelle's birthday. He had promised her dinner, then cocktails at Mr. Kelly's. She'll be here in a few minutes, he thought, I should get dressed. But Buyers was stalled. Something had happened to him in Florida, something he could not pinpoint. He didn't know why, but he certainly knew when he had first felt this way. It started on that hot sunny day when he and his companions went to visit the Crab Lady.

On the shell mound was a lean-to made from a tarp. The boy played underneath it as if he were playing in a sandbox. A red tree grew out of the center of the mound, hanging from the limbs were linen fishing nets and numbered cork floats painted bright yellow. Wooden crab traps were piled six high and four deep along a pier that extended forty or fifty feet into the water. The shack stood on stilts at the other end of the fishing pier. When they reached the shack that day the Crab Lady and her mate were waiting for them. The six-dozen crabs were ready. She greeted them and invited them in for a cool glass of fresh lemonade. Are you crazy? Don had thought as he surveyed the ramshackle hut in disgust. But when he entered the shack, he was amazed by its clean and orderly ambience.

He did not need to be a college professor to note the intelligence of form and function. The exposed rafters, plank pine floor, and large overhangs added to the design and kept the house cool. Open windows allowed the Gulf breeze to enter; it was a straightforward design uncomplicated by the dictates of convention. He felt a gnawing in his stomach, as though he was missing some silent message.

There were only two rooms, a large kitchen-living room area and a bedroom. Hanging upside down from the ceiling rafters were dried flowers and herbs. Hung along the sink were fishnets holding fruit, potatoes, and onions.

When the rest of his friends went outside to watch the Crab Lady cut the pinchers off the crabs, Buyers stayed inside and looked around. In the center of the room were a table and four chairs. The table was covered in a linen tablecloth. In the center was a kerosene lamp surrounded by red hibiscus flowers. A book lay open, its pages yellowed and curled. He could not resist the temptation and he turned the cover over, Tolkien's The Hobbit. For some reason, he was not surprised.

There were three chairs and a small sofa of some faded damask in the living room area. In the corner of the room was a three-foot-wide bookcase that went floor to ceiling. Like a magnet he gravitated to the shelves; again he was not surprised. A collection of Russian writers took a prominent place, Tolstoy, Pushkin, Pasternak, and Dostoyevsky. There were full sets of Shakespeare, Chaucer, and Churchill's WWII memoirs.

Buyers picked up Kafka's Metamorphosis, riffled the pages, and put it back on the shelf. There was a selection of fairy tales and nursery rhymes. He marveled at the collection of books crammed into a three-foot space.

He walked outside and watched the Crab Lady, with her tall elegance and severe hair pulled to that tight knot at the nap of her neck, and envied her squat companion. They worked well together. He was positive that they enjoyed a quality of life he lacked in Chicago.

The Crab Lady had an earthiness just like the girl in the Ice Cream Shop. What was her name? That's right, he remembered, Kate. She was not bad looking. She had a good, slim figure and red hair, not like copper, more like polished mahogany. He smiled. She had the devil in her brown eyes. He would have been attracted if she hadn't been so sarcastic. He could handle smart-ass men but not woman like her. She dared to tell him to his face that he had an alligator mouth and a canary ass. The women he knew in Chicago would not have insulted him in that manner. They were definitely more sophisticated, like Isabelle.

As if on cue, Isabelle came up behind him and put her arms around his still wet body. She played with his navel and then fingered the hairs on his stomach. She kissed his back, then worked her mouth down his spine and punctuated her teasing by biting his ass.

"You'll have to wait till later for the rest," she said.

"Make me a martini, a Tanqueray martini with a lemon twist."

He said this in a tone so cold and so demanding that she stared at his naked back and started to tell him to get it himself. But she bit her lip, went behind the bar, and fumbled with the glasses.

In the 1960's every city had it's rooms, sanctuaries of food and drink known only by city intimates. There's the Persian Room, the Zephyr Room, the Rainbow Room, and, in Chicago, the Pump Room.

Don tipped the maître de' his usual ten spot, and they were quickly escorted to their favorite table against the wall near the dance floor. The headwaiter greeted them promptly.

"Hello, Mr. Buyers. Good to see you this evening. Your usual?"

Don nodded.

"Would madam like the same?"

"Yes, except with an olive," Isabelle said.

He disappeared.

Isabelle opened her evening bag and took out a gold cigarette case. She extracted a Russian cigarette wrapped in green paper with a gold filter tip. After placing the cigarette in a gold cigarette holder, she waited for Don to light it.

He picked up the gold lighter she gave him for his birthday and did the honors. She took a long deep drag and blew the cigarette smoke out through her nose.

At that precise moment, something clicked. Suddenly he hated her. He hated her fake sophistication, her materialism, and her beauty. The sudden realization was so strong and came so quickly that he looked away and pretended to scan the restaurant for a familiar face. He knew the rest of the evening would be difficult.

The waiter from the bar came with their drinks. He wore a white satin Eton jacket embroidered in gold braid. On his head he wore the Pump Room headdress, a cap with plumed feathers that stood a foot high. In his hand he carried a sterling silver and crystal tray on which stood two tall crystal glasses containing two perfect Tanqueray martinis, one with an olive and the other with a lemon twist. The liquid was so clear one could see through it; a slight film of condensation collected on the outside of the glass. Buyers ran his tongue along the lip of the glass. The coldness on the tip of his tongue stirred some deep longing, a strange feeling he hadn't felt before. It gave him a sensuous power of unexplained magnitude.

"Cheers," Isabelle said.

"Happy Birthday. Oh, I have a present, a little something."

He pulled out of his jacket pocket a small wrapped jewelry box. Isabelle's face glowed; she instantly thought it was an engagement ring. Her fingers trembled, and she could hardly get the wrapping off the box.

Inside was a small gold circle pin encrusted with seed pearls and diamonds.

"The sales lady said circle pins are the latest."

Buyers said. "So, I bought the most elegant one they had. I hope you like the pin."

She sat staring at the pin. Isabelle was beautiful. She had natural blond hair and legs that did not stop. His friends envied him. But as Buyers embraced his new feelings toward her, he realized she lacked the pheromone that men didn't talk about, the ability to mentally fuck. She didn't engage his brain. And he realized that his gift, a brooch instead of an engagement ring, was just what she deserved.

*****

Rush Street, known for its nightclubs, fast women, and watered-down drinks, is a magnet for anyone seeking adventure and excitement. Rush Street is the place in Chicago where you can find or buy anything under the sun. The nightclub entertainment ranged from nude girls in birdcages to jazz clubs with the greatest jazz musician, to discos and Mr. Kelly's, which always has the latest and hottest in entertainment.

On the corner of Rush and Oak Street, Don and Isabelle sat in traffic. A fender bender at the intersection had brought traffic to a standstill. Buyers considered leaving the car and walking the block to Mr. Kelly's. But it was so damn cold that he decided to wait it out. As he sat there, he watched the night people go in and out of the Oak Street Market, an all-night grocery store featuring gourmet food and rare wines. Steam rose from the manhole covers, pirouetted, and then dissipated in the freezing air.

Isabelle sat next to him. He knew she was disappointed; she had expected a ring. Now that he realized he hated her she would never receive that ring, not from him anyway. When he found Isabelle, she was a virgin. He taught her well, now she was a damn nymphomaniac. Their lovemaking was very passionate but hardly euphoric. Tonight he understood how much he disliked her and why. She could be bought. Like tonight, he bought her with a fucking gold pin.

A prostitute illegally parked her white Cadillac in front of the store. Leaving the motor running, she jumped out of the car wearing a full-length white mink coat. She ran into the market and reappeared a few minutes later carrying what seemed like a bottle of wine in a brown paper bag.

Buyers felt a tightness in his pants and reached over to Isabelle. He touched the back of her neck and beckoned her.

"No."

"No one will see. The windows are steamed."

She looked around and shook her head no. But he was determined. He put a little more pressure on the back of her neck and he gently pushed her head down on him. He watched the steam escape from the manhole covers, and then he noticed the condensation on the windshield start to drip. He tried to remember where he had seen condensation drip like that before. Then he remembered; that smart-mouthed woman in an ice cream shop in Florida.

The Price of Crabs

*****

The ropes were out again along Michigan Avenue, to keep people from being blown into traffic. Buyers always found it amusing to watch people fight the wind as it blew through the streets between the tall skyscrapers like Santa Ana gusts through narrow canyons.

He stood across from the United Insurance Building and watched the crane maneuver white marble slabs up the side of the structure. He scrutinized the workers as they set the marble in place with great care and precision.

The slim sixty-story edifice of white marble and black tinted windows would be a dynamic skyscraper, a credit to the Chicago skyline, with its geometric form, a sharp contrast to the wedding cake design of the Wrigley Building just a block away.

He was jealous. The committee rejected the design his firm had submitted. He blamed it on politics and told himself that his design was far superior. But he knew, down inside, that his vision was inferior.

He left the building site, walked down Michigan Avenue, took a right on Chicago Avenue, and headed for Navy Pier. It was a long walk. But today he needed the exercise and the flagellation of the crisp air. When he turned east on Chicago Avenue, the full force of the wind coming off the lake took his breath away.

He pulled the collar of his black cashmere overcoat

up around his ears, lowered his head into his chest, and walked briskly toward the lake. As he neared Lake Michigan the wind became colder, as if driving the lake's freezing waters slashing across his face until it brought tears to his eyes and froze the hairs in his nose.

When he finally reached Navy Pier, the buildings blocked the wind. But Buyers didn't take refuge on the lee side of the buildings. Instead, he walked to the end of the pier.

He stood alone on the pier on that gray miserable day in Chicago. What a terrible thing it is to reach middle age and realize that you will never be any more than you are, he thought. Mediocrity was a word he loathed. But he knew he would never design a building like the United Insurance Building. He lacked that one ingredient that makes a man a genius, imagination. He was mechanically a great engineer. He could design anything, allowing for weight bearing, degrees of stress, and angles. But he lacked creative imagination, and that one missing ingredient made him mediocre. The last two days were a powerful self-realization for him, and he didn't like the conclusions.

So he watched the gray breakers of Lake Michigan hit the pier and the water spray over the cement pilings. He stood a long time facing into the wind, letting the harsh spray flay his face. As he watched the whitecaps roll, he seemed to hear four words carried on the waves: "alligator mouth canary ass."

He lit an English Oval with his wind-proof lighter and sucked it with vicious ecstasy, like a man biting a woman's nipple for pain and pleasure. He inhaled deep into his lungs and exhaled slowly. As the smoke left his lungs, it carried with it all his fears. Buyers threw the unfinished cigarette into the lake and watched it bob about before it submerged.

He turned and faced the magnificent skyline of Chicago. He made his decision and walked slowly toward his destiny with the wind at his back.

*****

Isabelle roamed the streets of Brooklyn looking for interesting shops, places to eat, and cute boutiques. Her interview at Abraham Strauss Department Store went well. She felt confident that she would get the job. Brooklyn is not that much different than Chicago. After Buyers left for Florida she was desponded. He made it perfectly clear that there was no room for her in his life. She loved him, although she knew it was hopeless. When he said, "I do not love you." And that he felt no obligation toward her. She felt her world came to an abrupt stop

"You can find a job and get an apartment. I am leaving for Florida in the next few days and my conscience would be clear if I had no obligations to you." He said facing the window.

"I thought we had a commitment."

"I know, I know, but you know how I am, here today and gone tomorrow."

"I don't need your help."

"Suit yourself. Now, about a martini and some dinner for old time sake?"

"No, I feel a little sick. I think I will leave, now."

She picked up her purse and coat and made a slow retreat. When she closed the door, she became sick to her stomach and started crying all at the same time. She felt so ashamed and used. I would have done anything for him. She thought. I was seventeen when I started dating him; I have not seen anyone since. He was my life. I could have sworn we would have gotten married. I feel used somehow, I feel dirty, and unclean. To be dismissed just like that. Like I was some servant. Maybe I was. I will show him that I can get along without him. I left Chicago didn't I?

Now, walking the streets of Brooklyn, she was thinking, I still don't feel comfortable about myself. No matter how many times I go to church I still feel unclean. Give it time I tell myself. It has been months and still I don't want to date and the thought of getting involved with another man makes me sick to my stomach. Distracted and a little numb, saw a cute shop and walked inside.

*****

It was Monday afternoon and Jerry just finished some agonizing paper work. He threw the pencil down on his desk.

"That's that, till next month, anyway."

The Price of Crabs

He pushed his chair back, brought his legs up and cross them on his desk. Grabbed his cigarettes, lit one and took a long, deep satisfying drag. He then blew the smoke in a fine long line. He watched the smoke slowly ascend and disperse in the air. He concentrated on his business. He owned and managed this gym. He made a decent living. Not as much money as when he was in the ring. He missed the fighting. He liked the excitement, especially the notoriety, the entourage of people, the nightlife, the booze, and the women. That's it, the women. Mmmmm. He loved women. Women always got him in trouble, especially beautiful women.

"Yes," He said out loud. Beautiful women were the reason for my divorce. There were so many when I was fighting, now I hardly have a dinner date. He stood up walked to the window. He unlocked the window and lifted it up and drank in the musty air. There is something alive about air, even when it smells of street, vendor's wares, gasoline, and human beings. He thought about moving. Maybe to Florida where the air is clean and crisp and the smell of salt water is refreshing. But, he had a daughter in a private school and he did not want the upheaval of moving so close to his divorce.

"Not a bad day, considering." He said to no one.

He stood there and watched the action down on the street. His gym was on the second floor over a retail store and he liked the street. He watched the people mingle and he watched them go in and out of the shops. He waved at Mr. Fischer across the street. He owns a small grocery store and kept his fruit in baskets in front of the store, tempting people to buy them as they looked so fresh and delectable. Jerry loved Granny Smith Green Apples and every morning he would purchase himself two apples. He and Mr. Fischer would banter back and forth over the freshness of the fruit.

He lit another cigarette and smoked it casually.

He watched the people on the street below and listen to the cars stop and go. When he caught is breadth, there she was a tall blonde in a blue dress, slender but not skinny, he dislike skinny hard body women. He liked them soft and cuddly with some flesh on them. He notice she a had a slight ever so small stomach. "I like that, " he thought. I would like to run my hand all over that belly

"Yes." He said.

He watched her walk along the sidewalk. She was looking into the shop windows as though she had all day. She reached Fischer's Grocery and stopped and looked at the fruit. He thought she was deciding between an apple and a peach. He turned and grabbed the Granny Smith off his desk.

"Hey you. You in the blue dress." He yelled.

Isabelle turned and looked around and then she looked up. There was this big, ugly man hanging out the window.

"Catch." He said and threw the apple.

To her surprise she caught it.

"Good Catch." He said.

She waved her hand at him, the one that held the apple and mouthed "Thank you."

The Price of Crabs

Jerry waved his hand, closed the window and turned away and sat down at his desk. "Why did I do that?" He asked himself. "Why did I close the window?" He felt stupid and a little strange. He lit another cigarette. Then he smoked two more. He found that his hand was shaking. He forced himself up from his desk and went back to the window. She was gone. Jerry looked both up and down the street but there was no sight of her.

Stump Pass - 1979

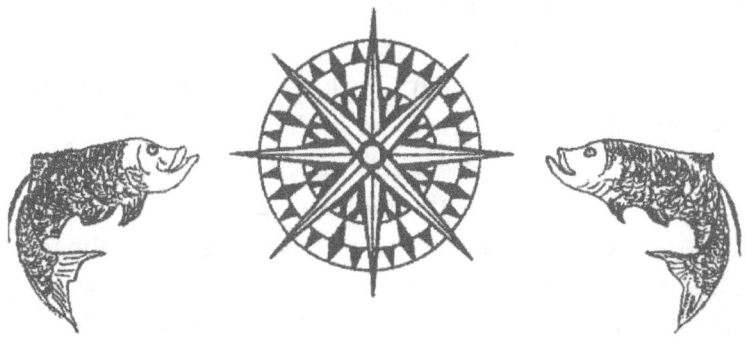

A Bulldozer, Fishermen, and an Ugly Man

*T*he best months in Florida are spring and fall. The air is crisp, the humidity is low, and the sky is the most beautiful cerulean.

On a beautiful Saturday morning, the first day of November, Kate's son, Steven, decided to go fishing. Like a good mother she packed him a lunch, gave him several bottles of water, and walked with him to the boat dock. She wished him well with the old mantra of mothers, "be careful." She stood on the dock and watched him maneuver the waterway until he was in the bay.

Then he opened up the engine, took off like a flash, and was gone.

Kate walked back to the ice cream shop and started her morning chores. She refilled the hot fudge warmer, ice cream cone dispenser, and the napkin holders. Then she started replacing the ice cream in the cooler. As she rummaged through the freezer pulling out the five-gallon tub of vanilla ice cream, a great boom rattled the windows and shook everything in the shop.

"What the hell was that?" she wondered. Then the sound came again, this time louder. Kate recognized the sound but couldn't place it. Instinctually she ran for the front door. Outside on the shell drive, several people watched as a giant bulldozer was off-loaded from a barge on Shell Creek. Kate walked up to a group of men standing around and asked what was going on.

"We're bulldozing the old turpentine shacks today."

"What?"

"You heard me, miss. Those shacks will be gone by noon. The property has been sold and the new owner doesn't want them, they're in the way."

Before she could digest this information, Kate heard her name.

At the door of the Ice Cream Shop stood the four fishermen who usually stopped by every morning for coffee.

"Do you have the coffee on or do I have to go home and drink my wife's dishwater?" yelled Dwayne.

"It's on."

"Good," said Harold. The four of them scrambled

into the shop and took their seats at their usual table.

"Do any of you know what is going on?" Kate asked as she served them.

"Well," Harold announced. "I have a cousin that works for the county zonin' office and the scuttlebutt is that a corporation out of Miami purchased all the property from Shell Creek to the Pass. Now they're waitin for, what you call it, a PUD?"

He explained to Kate that the sale was contingent on whether their building plan was approved. She realized that the county was so strapped for cash that the commissioners would probably jump at the chance to see some new tax revenue.

"What is a PUD? It sounds like a contraceptive," snickered Dwayne.

"Dwayne, you some kind of moron? A PUD stands for Plan Unit Development. You thinkin' of that thing your momma should have used before she had you, an IUD. Sometimes I think you are dumber than a box of rocks."

"Look here Harold, I ain't no moron, and I ain't dumber than a box of rocks," Dwayne smirked. He chewed on the ever-present cigar wedged in the side of his mouth. Dwayne was never without it; he talked, ate, maybe even slept with it in his mouth. When he got excited while talking, he sprayed tobacco juice from the corners of his mouth. "I can hear and speak jus' fine." Dwayne rolled the cigar to the other side of his mouth." What's the difference between an IUD and PUD? Nothin', cause with either one some-body's gonna get fucked."

Russ chuckled. "Ain't that right, boy? In this world it's all about sex and money. You either the fucker or the fuckee and I am usually one of the -ees."

"Go ahead, fool," Chappie spoke up. "What else do you know, Harold?"

"It's supposed to be kept quiet until everything is approved. The PUD showed a marina with a restaurant surrounded by condominiums. Each condo gets a boat slip. Plus they'll be extra slips for boaters 'cause the restaurant will be accessible by water. Across the street from the marina will be an eighteen-hole golf course surrounded by homes. I'm not sure 'bout the rest of the development."

"Whooee," Chappie said. He was a dead ringer for Mr. Clean; he always wore white painter pants and a white T-shirt. As bald as a cucumber and sporting a small white goat-tee, Chappie was usually the butt of the men's jokes. He had recently started hanging with a girl half his age, a firebrand who kept him hopping.

"Yup," Harold continued. Now that he was the center of attention, he milked it for all it was worth. Harold always dressed and acted as if he was looking for a better job. He always wore a pressed cotton shirt and clean khaki trousers; never any spots or dirt marks despite his hours spent on the water. "My cousin said they purchased all the land from the Pass to the Gulf of Mexico. There's talk about some street going through. She said that the wooden bridges would be replaced and made higher so boat traffic could go under them and open up all the land and waterways on the other side of the bridges. There was talk about the point being sold."

"What point?" Kate asked.

Harold answered. "You don't know about the point? How long you been livin' here?

"Not long enough, I guess."

"On the other side of the shacks is a sweet parcel of land, it goes all the way to the bay and has a shell beach. I cannot believe you never been there. You should a take a walk. Get out of the Ice Cream Shop, Kate, and do a little explorin'."

"Harold, I guess I will have to do, just that."

At that moment Steven burst into the shop carrying a stringer of three large fish.

"Look what I caught," he crowed.

Kate and the men all looked at the fish. They were huge, probably twenty-thirty inches long, nice and fat, just right for dinner.

"Those are redfish, son," Dwayne said. "You can tell by the black dot on the side near their tail. Where did you catch them?

"In the Bay, there was a hole. I threw a line in and I got a bite right away. I threw another line in and a second fish bit right off. I bet there were twenty or thirty fish in that hole."

"Where in the bay?" asked Russ.

"You know where Wash Ally comes close to the sand bar? You know the sand bar where we dig for clams?"

All of the fishermen nodded.

"Why didn't you catch more fish?" Kate asked.

"Because I was so excited, I never saw a fish this big

and I wanted to show them to you," the boy bragged.

"Steve, they are great. I'll help you filet them and I'll cook them for supper, okay?"

"Yeah."

"What kind of bait did you use?" Russ asked.

"Fresh shrimp."

"And they took it right off?"

"Yeah."

The fishermen looked from one to the other. They all stood up at the same time, fished through their pockets, threw some money down on the table, and left quickly.

"Have a nice day, Kate," Dwayne called out.

Kate started clearing the coffee cups and was surprised they had left a tip. They never had before.

"I guess they are going to find your fishing hole, Steve."

"That's okay, Mom."

As Kate was clearing the coffee cups from the table; the Ice Cream Shop door open and a big ugly man entered.

"I was told this is the place for good ice cream."

"You were told right." Kate answered.

"My name is Jerry."

"I am Kate or Kathryn, never call me Katie."

"I like that, a women with boundaries."

"Would you like some ice cream?"

"I understand you have good coffee."

"That I do."

"I'll have coffee then."

"Cream and sugar?"

"Nope, I like my coffee like my women, hot, dark, and strong."

"You mean black, hot, and sassy?" Kate replied.

"That, too."

"I like a man without boundaries," Kate flirted

The man just laughed. "I like them funny like you, sister,"

"Okay." Kate laughed, enjoying his sense of humor. She poured him a cup of coffee and handed it to him. He remained standing at the cooler; he didn't take a seat at a table. Kate watched him for a moment as he rested his elbows on top of the cooler. He was tall.

As if reading her mind, he spoke up. "Six foot five inches."

"Are you a mind reader?"

"Of sorts, I have many talents."

"I see. Are you new to the area?" Kate asked.

"Two days."

"Where are you from and what brings you to Florida?"

"I'm from Brooklyn, I like the air."

"You don't have a Brooklyn accent. You sound more like a Midwesterner," Kate answered

"Well, where do you think I'm from?"

"Hmm, I may be wrong, but I think you are from the mid-west, Cleveland."

"What are you a mind reader?"

"Of sorts, I have many talents."

He laughed. Kate noticed that when he smiled, he wasn't so ugly. He reached into his breast pocket and pulled out a cigarette and lighter.

"I don't allow smoking in here. The smoke gets in the ice cream. Anyway you should quit."

"I didn't see a 'no smoking sign.' I don't go where I can't smoke."

"I am sorry, but the sign is over that door. You must have missed it when you walked in." Kate pointed to the door and the sign.

He turned and looked at the sign, shrugged his shoulders, and put the cigarette back into his pocket.

"If I quit, would it improve my good looks?"

"I don't know," Kate said, liking him even more. "Let's see, turn your head to the left."

He did.

"Now, turn your head to the right."

He did.

"Well?" he asked.

"No, I don't think quitting smoking will make you handsome, maybe healthier, but not handsomer. Sorry."

He gulped down the rest of his coffee and put the empty cup on top of the cooler. He turned and started for the door. Kate was beginning to feel guilty until he put a bill on the counter and with a big smile.

"Catch you later, Katie."

Zing! She smiled.

*****

She was fairly busy the rest of the day. The bulldozing stopped around one o'clock and the workers came in for lunch. At least this meant some business,

Kate thought. But as much as she pumped them for information the less they seemed to know. All she got was the same news Harold had delivered earlier in the day. But what does this all mean? How many acres are there? How many units? How many people? When will they begin and when will they finish? Do I want to live next to condos? Kate had moved to her corner of Nowheresville to get away from people, not to be surrounded by them.

Steven interrupted her thoughts.

"Mom, is it okay if Philip and I go fishing again? The tide goes out in about an hour and maybe I'll catch some more redfish."

"Sure, Steve." Then she thought a moment. "Steve, tell me, have you ever been to the Point?"

"All the time, I catch fiddler crabs and sell them to Bob at the bait shop. He sells them to the fishermen. You can't believe the amount of fiddler crabs out there, I bet there are thousands. Oh, and another thing, you should see the quail."

"How come I've never been out there?"

"I don't know, but you should go, Mom, you'd love it."

"Just be careful and don't run into any sand bars," Kate said. "I think I'll close up early and got take a look at the Point"

"You be careful, Mom." He laughed and was out the door in a second.

"Be back by supper, Steve," Kate shouted after him."

Kate put the GONE FISHING sign on the door. Then she walked outside and down the shell drive out to the street. There wasn't a soul in either direction. The street was deserted. It was only four o'clock and everyone was in their roost. It was still hot for November but the humidity was low.

I cannot believe that this is the first time I am walking to the point, Kate thought, I have lived here almost two years. Now, when it's about to be destroyed, I'm discovering it. Kate noticed the workers had piled all the debris from the shacks in several mounds. They had knocked over a lot trees and they were also in piles. The ground in places was scraped down to the bare earth. It looked horrible. Kate romanticized about the shacks. The dark gray clapboard houses with faded and peeling paint. They looked nostalgic, especially with the over grown weeds and flowers. A whole past had been wiped out in less than four hours. In ten years no one would remember there was a turpentine camp along Turtle Creek. The people who lived here distilling pine tar into turpentine will be forgotten, she thought, and their memories scattered like these piles of debris.

Practical considerations pulled her out of her reverie. Kate realized that she was lost. "Where is that path?" she asked out loud. "I should have asked Steven for directions."

Then out of nowhere there was a cut in the palmettos. As she stepped into the woods the temperature dropped at least 10 to 20 degrees. The shade and coolness was a pleasant surprise. I don't need my sunglasses," she thought, as she began to focus on the flora around her.

There was canopy made up of tall pines, live oaks,

scrub oaks, wax myrtles, Australian pines and very tall palms, along with a variety of trees Kate didn't recognize. She could see the blue sky through a lacework of leaves. In front of her was a very old live oak tree, its adulating branches reached out into the forest at least fifty feet. The trunk was at least ten feet in diameter. Running through its foliage were gray squirrels, and several scrub jays chasing the squirrels from tree to tree. A mocking bird and a woodpecker led the chorus of songbirds. The wind whistled through the Australian pines in contrapuntal refrains. The forest floor was covered wall to wall with palmettos. As she walked through them she heard what she hoped were lizards, not snakes, scurrying.

Leaving the forest, Kate stumbled across a salt flat. To the north was a sandy beach with thousands of fiddler crabs whose clicking reminded her of a swarm of locusts. Steven was right when he said thousands, Kate thought. Beyond the beach with the crabs was nothing but water with a mangrove island here and there. To the south was a sandy beach with a view of water all the way to the Harbor. To the West lay a thicket of mangroves. As she walked through a cut in the mangroves out to very tip of the point Kate, had an unobstructed view of the Bay to Wash Alley.

She didn't have to be a genius to know that she was looking at a million-dollar view with the Bay, Wash Alley and beyond to the blue-green waters of the Gulf of Mexico. It was not hard to imagine builders trucking in loads of sand to expand this area. She could see developers clearing out the mangroves and building a tiki bar.

"I can almost hear the sound of a steel-drum band playing Caribbean music and the smell of rum punches and margaritas," she told the universe.

"Hi Lady, talkin' to yourself?"

Kate froze in her tracks. She slowly turned around and there stood Jerry.

"What are you doing here?"

"I might ask you the same thing."

"I am exploring this beautiful place before someone destroys it forever."

"And, who might that be?"

"I don't know, I just heard today that some person bought the land and is planning to build condos." She explained.

"Not anymore," Jerry pointed south to a stand of high pine trees. "There's an eagle's nest over there and they are protected by law." And sure enough there at the top was a nest.

"As long as that nest stays in use no one can disturb it. Law says you have to leave twenty-five acres around it undisturbed while the birds are nesting."

"Good! Since eagles have a long life, say thirty or forty years; that is longer then you or I will live so the eagles get to frolic and the condos go on hold."

"You got somethin' against progress?"

"No," Kate pouted. "But I have a lot against destruction."

"There is nothing here to destroy."

"There is everything to destroy," Kate disputed. "How long do you think it took that live oak to grow? What about that fat pine tree with the eagle's nest in it? No one can replace this once it is gone. Build condos, put in roads, parking lots, etc. etc. and all this pristine beautiful land is gone forever. Oh, it would make someone very wealthy if you multiply twenty-five condos an acre by what, $100,000, maybe more like $150,000 each? How many acres are here? That is lot of money. And, who benefits from it all, a few snowbirds that can afford to stay at a fancy resort. Certainly the county will gain tax revenue. With growth and civilization you lose a certain amount of freedom, and the environment around you gives up some of its natural beauty."

""That's some speech. You have definite views for an ice cream lady." He took out his cigarettes again. "May I smoke?"

"Yes, of course."

Suddenly Kate's boys hoved into view. "Hey Mom, we caught some trout." Steven shouted as he and Philip rounded the point. Steve cut the motor and slid the boat onto the beach. Phil threw out the anchor and they both jumped out, Phil carrying a stringer of four or five trout.

"Where did you guys catch those fish?" Jerry asked.

"In the grass flats." Steve answered.

"Looks like good eating."

"Speaking of eating, we better get home," Kate said. "By the time we filet those fish and I start cooking..."

"Would you like some fish?" Steve asked Jerry.

"You said they were trout? I have never eaten trout

caught in salt water."

"Well, here is your chance." Steve took two trout from the stringer; put them in the pail of water he had in the boat, and gave the stringer with the rest of the fish to Jerry.

"You know how to filet fish?" asked Steven.

"I was a good Boy Scout," Jerry said. "Thank you."

"Just bring back the stringer," Steve yelled as he and Philip headed back to the boat.

"Mom, are you going to walk back or do you want a ride?"

"I think I would like a boat ride about now."

"Get on board, Mom." "Enjoy the fish."   Steve waved to Jerry.

"I owe you one, Steve." Jerry yelled.

Steve shook his head no and opened up the engine and off they went. It was tide change and the water laid back smooth like glass. Pelicans stood silently on their perch and not a sound could be heard except for the hum of Steve's motor as it cut a clear path through the bay waters toward Shell Creek and home.

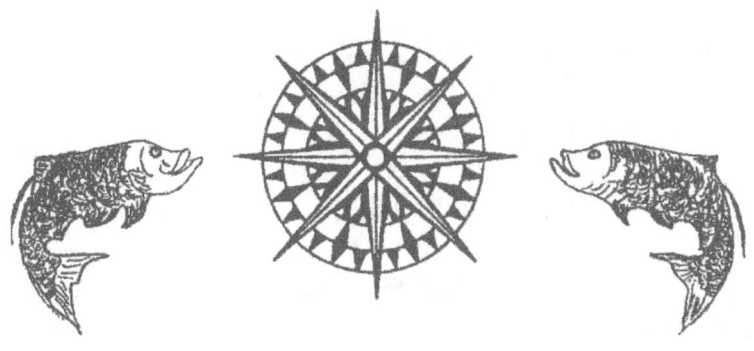

Mr Alligator Returns

*T*he phone rang and Philip answered it. "Hey Mom, you have a phone call from a Don Buyers."

"Who?" Kate asked as she walked back into the house from the ice cream shop. "Don Buyers? I don't know a Don Buyers."

"Well, he knows you," Philip said, as he handed Kate the phone.

"Probably a new boyfriend," Steve commented in the background. Kate shook her head, annoyed at her two sons.

"Hello?"

"Is this Kathryn Callahan?" a female voice asked.

"Yes."

"This is Isabelle, Don Buyers' secretary. I am calling because there will be a meeting next Thursday morning at ten o'clock; we are inviting everyone who may be affected by our new project. We want to familiarize you with our intentions and our concepts for this area."

"What project?"

"Don Buyers is the operating manager for our new housing project just south of the Turtle Creek Bridge; we just installed a new sign at the road."

"Wait a minute, what does this all have to do with me? I don't know a Don Buyers."

"I am sorry miss, but my instructions were to contact you. Mr. Buyers wants you to attend. It is important being that you own the ice cream shop. There will be other people there from the area and some county officials will be present. Mr. Buyers also mentioned there might be a position for you in this building project."

"Position?" Now Kate was really bemused. "I will try and make the meeting." She hung up the phone and turned to the kids.

"I don't know a Don Buyers."

"You sure he is not a new boyfriend and your just holding out?" Steve commented again.

"Steve…"

"If he is a new boyfriend make sure he has money; I'm going to need transportation soon, like a new car. Got it, Mom, like a car? You know, like four wheels?"

"Steve, go for a boat ride, just get out of here."

"Did you hear that, Philip? Let's go!" With that, both boys ran out of the house. "See you

"Be home before dark."

Steve and Phil were in the boat and down the waterway before Kate had time to think.

"Where are we going?" Phil asked his older brother.

"I don't know, but let's explore a little bit. Let's check out that new development. I heard they were off loading dirt movers today at school. I am not sure exactly where; but I have a hunch."

The two boys coasted south. The water was still with a little chop. Steve did not have his engine cranked all the way; he was searching. As he approached the Crab Lady's dock he realized his search was over. She and her mate were standing at the end of their dock and they looked fairly angry. Her boat dock extended forty to sixty feet into the bay; Steven put his engine in idle as he drew closer. Both he and Philip waved and yelled "hello." The angry couple waved back.

Opposite the Crab Lady's dock a barge was off-loading equipment. A group of men on the opposite shore were carrying tools for heavy equipment from the barge down a gangplank and back again. They carried a variety of things, most of which were unfamiliar to Steven.

He saw Harold, the fisherman that always came in to the ice cream shop for coffee, the same guy that fished out his redfish spot.

Without hesitation he pulled his boat along the shore.

Philip threw out the anchor and both boys jumpd ashore.

"Hi, Harold." Steve called. Harold turned around and saw the kids.

"Hey Steve how's the fishing? Have you caught anymore redfish?"

"Not since you and your buddies fished out that hole, the one I told you about."

"Yep, we sure did," the man, said with no shame. "How's your mom?"

"OK. You need a hand with any of this stuff?" Steve headed toward the barge, of course Philip followed.

"No, I think we have it covered."

As Harold answered Steve a tall man walked up. "Do you know these kids?" he asked Harold.

"Yeah, they belong to Kate, Kate Callahan, the ice cream lady."

"Really?" He walked up to the kids. "I am Don, who might you be?"

"I'm Steve and this is my brother Philip."

"Did I hear you say you wanted to help?"

"Yes, you did."

"Can you drive a truck?"

"I been driving a tractor since I was eight," Steve boasted

"What about you?" Don asked Philip.

"Me, I have been driving since I was five." Philip gave everyone a big smile as Steve rolled his eyes.

"Yeah, in your last reincarnation," Steve poked fun of his brother.

Don smiled. 'Peas in a pod', he thought. He turned

and pointed to a pile of stakes that were stacked on the ground. "Would you boys put them in the bed of that pick-up truck and bring them to Jim on the other side of the island?"

"Sure."

Steven and Philip followed Don to the pile of stakes. They both grabbed an armful and followed Don to where the pick-up truck was parked.

"Oh boy, is this a beauty. Where did you find this truck?" Steve placed the stakes in the bed of the truck and slowly surveyed the vehicle. He walked around it, running his hand along the fenders. Then he just stood in front of the truck and admired it. The old, beat-up green Chevy pick-up had a short wooden bed. It was not new by any means, but Steven was in love. He peeked in through the driver's side window and gasped. It had a long gearshift from the floor passed the bench seat.

"How old is this truck?"

"I believe it is a 1956 Chevy." Don replied. "We found it on the property when I purchased the land."

"Boy, would I love to have this! Where do you want us to drop the stakes?"

Don gave them direction and the kids took off bouncing along the sand dunes on their way to find Jim. Don went back to watch them finish the unloading of the barge. When he caught Harold's eye, he walked over to him. "Tell me about those kids."

"Well the youngest one I don't know too well, but the oldest is something else," Harold said. "They moved here about a year or two ago. Kate opened the ice cream shop and the boys and I started to go for coffee in the morning. You know, my wife makes the worst coffee. Well anyway, the kid had a hundred and fifty bucks in his pocket that he earned from a paper route up north; so he buys a seventeen-foot fiberglass boat. He's all excited and puts the boat in the water and it sinks; it had a hole in it. Well instead of getting down in the mouth. He pulls the boat out of the water, drags it over to the Landings and starts to work on it. He fixes the hole, sands it down, paints it a pretty color, puts a 'for sale' sign on it and sells the thing for two hundred and fifty bucks."

Don raised his eyebrows.

"He then finds an aluminum flats boat for a hundred and fifty bucks. He goes over to Chuck's Marina and tells Chuck he wants to buy a boat motor. Chuck shows him a five hundred-dollar Johnson Outboard Motor. Steven gives him a hundred dollars he made from the sale of the fiberglass boat and asks Chuck if he could work the rest off."

"He sounds like a real wheeler-dealer," Buyers stated.

"That's not the half of it," Harold went-on. "Chuck says he has some crab traps that need to be put together; a dollar a trap. He then says, Steve could work some odds and end jobs, for three-dollars an hour. Steve says OK. But, Chuck wouldn't give him the motor until he paid it off. Steve wanted it right then and there. Chuck says, 'Let me think about this some; come back tomorrow after school and I will let you know. Anyway, Chuck went and talked to Kate, that's Steve's mom, and she offered to sign a note for the money if the boy doesn't come through.

"Is that a fact," Buyers mused.

"They're good people," Harold said. "She made Chuck promise not to tell Steve, an' that boy spent almos' a half year workin' that bill off."

Buyers nodded, and filed that information away.

*****

Steve and Phil were in their glory bouncing along the sand dunes in the green pick-up truck. As they came around a dune they saw a man with red hair and a red beard placing stakes. He looked up saw the pick-up truck and yelled, "Over here."

The boys drove to where Jim was standing, turned off the motor, and jumped out. "Put the stakes over there in a pile." As Jim gave directions he never took his eyes off his work, he just pointed.

Phil gave Steve a shrug and did what the man told them to do.

"Is that all?" Philip asked. Jim waved his hand, nodded, and went back to what he was doing.

"Oh well." Steve shrugged his shoulders, as he got back into the pick-up and looked at Phil. "He is one strange dude."

"I don't think he takes any wooden nickels."

They returned to where the group of men was still standing. The barge was pulling away from the shore. Steve parked the truck where he found it. He and his brother walked down to the shore and he gave the keys back to Don.

The Crab Lady was still standing on her dock watching the barge leave. She looked very concerned.

"She's not a happy camper." Steve observed.

"She just lost her view." Philip made a wise cracked.

"She does not like the barge coming in here." Don mentioned. "It disturbs the crab traps."

"You know there's a cut in the mangroves a few hundred feet north of that dock and there is another cut on this side further up."

Buyers turned and gave Steven a sharp look. "Really? How far up would you say?"

The boy repeated the directions, and then motioned to his brother. "Phil, I think it's time to go home."

"Nice meeting you two," Don said

"See ya," Harold said. "Say hey to your mom for me."

The boys got back into their boat. Steve started the motor and they soon headed up the waterway.

Don looked at the Crab Lady. He knew he had a problem. Then he looked back at the kids in the boat and started to smile. Steve pointed to the right, went further north, and then pointed to the left and waved good-bye. Then he gunned the motor, put the boat up on plane, and took off like a jet.

Don's smile grew larger till his lips curled on both sides and he chuckled out load. "That kid just saved me a lawsuit."

Steven and Philip walked into the door, just as Kate

pulled baked trout from the oven.

"Just in time," She put dinner on the table. While they ate Steve filled Kate in on their adventure,

"Another carpetbagger," Kate said as she turned up her nose.

"What do you mean by carpetbagger?" Steve asked.

"He's an opportunist," Phil broke in. "I learned that word in history class."

"I don't think so, I think he has integrity," Steve said.

"Why, because he knew you were under age and he let you drive that pick-up all over the island?" Kate asked.

"No, Mom, I have a good feeling about him."

"He wants that pick-up, can't you tell." Philip smiled. "Harold was there, he might be workin' for Don Buyers."

With that Kate started clearing the table. She told the boys to finish and went into the ice cream shop for the evening shift. As she walked away she could hear Steven say. "I have to figure out a trade, I don't have anything to trade."

"You could always steal it."

"I thought of that, but that wouldn't work, not with my luck I'd probably end in jail." They laughed. "I can just see Mom now."

"Big Bro, you have a problem."

"I have to figure this out, you know he owes me one, I showed him the cut in the mangroves. He was worried about the Crab Lady. He just may owe me big time, I just have to find a way to approach him."

Carolyn Siemon Schöner

$$*****$$

Don Buyers sat behind his desk twirling a gold Cross-pen between his fingers. He was digesting the events of the day. So those are Kate's boys, he thought. I like them. The oldest is something else again. Anyone tenacious enough to spend several months making crab traps to pay off his boat motor certainly is determined. He didn't have to show me those cuts. He wants that pick-up truck. I could just make a gift of the truck. He knows I owe him and I'll bet my last dollar he is trying to figure out a way to own that truck. The truck cost me nothing, but finding a place to build a dock could save me millions in leases, franchises, and lawyer's fees.

He stood up and went over to the window. He smiled. I am just going to sit back and let him make the first move, I guarantee Steve has a plan, Buyers thought. Whatever his proposal I'll let him squirm a little, then give him the pick-up.

He thought a little bit more about the younger boy. He's sharp. Right away he saw my problem with the Crab Lady. I like that. I'll talk to Jim about those cuts when he gets back from the island. If we can use them, we can build our own dock big enough to maneuver a barge.

That Crab Lady. Buyers shook his head. Shit, she was seething today. I admire her. I like what she stands for; she has more dignity and sophistication in over-all's and yellow fishing boots than the Queen of England has in Buckingham Palace. She's like Kate, that ice cream lady, except Kate is vulnerable; I can get to her though her children. But that Crab Lady? Yeah, I like the idea of using the cuts Steven told me about. The longer I delay a confrontation with the Crab Lady the better. Okay, he thought, let's roll.

"Isabelle," he yelled. "Could you come in here?"

Isabelle sashayed into Don's office smoking one of her green cigarettes.

"Two things, please let me know when Jim gets back from the key, I want to talk to him. And make arrangements for me to go to Chicago next week. I've decided not to be present at the meeting, Jim and Gunter can handle it."

"You're going to Chicago?"

"Yes," he said, relishing the chance to hurt her. "You will stay here."

"Oh," mumbled a disappointed Isabelle."

"Tell Rose in Chicago to set up a meeting with our surveyors and engineers for the same day I get back," Buyers snapped. "Have her call Harold Greenberg, ask him to meet me for drinks at the Whitehall at around six. Let me know the times that Rose has scheduled these appointments."

Isabelle took down the final bit of information, paused, and then took a long drag on her cigarette.

"And look, please don't smoke in here, I detest the smell since I quit smoking. Now go and finish that cigarette." As an afterthought Don added. "When you come back make us a couple of martinis, I'll have mine on the rocks."

She left and he could hear the front door slam shut.

*****

Jim scratched on the door outside of Don's office, "You wanted to see me?"

"Come in," Don cut to the chase. "Do you know about a cut or an inlet just north of the Crab Lady?"

"Yep, there is old dock and a small lagoon. Why?"

"One of the boys pointed it out today."

"The older one, I see him on the water all the time. He knows the bay waters like the back of his hand," Jim said.

"Let's check it out tomorrow. One more thing—I'm going to Chicago and I'll miss the meeting next week. Will you take over for me? You're contractor on record anyway, that makes you the boss of all construction. I want you to offer Kate Callahan a position in design. Tell her we need someone to be a consultant, some kind of bullshit; you know the program well enough. We probably won't need her for a year or two. We haven't broken ground yet."

Jim stood nodding his head in agreement. "About tomorrow, we'll take my mullet boat in case we hit shallow water. I can handle the meeting. Who is Kate Callahan?"

"She is about to lose her business," Buyers smirked. "She just doesn't know it yet. But just ask around, she's the ice cream lady.

"What time Thursday? Not too early"

"The meeting is scheduled for ten in the morning."

"Okay, boss, if that is all, I'll see you in the morning." Jim left.

Don wanted that meeting to show Miss Uppity Kate that he had the power, money, and influence to rock her world. He had wanted to watch the expression on her face when the officials announced the destruction of the bridges, the closing of roads, and end of her business. Who had the alligator mouth now? He'd ask her. But meeting her boys had softened his opinion of the ice cream lady. He felt he owed some loyalty to Steven and Philip. We can put off the announcement till I get back from Chicago.

He was smiling when Isabelle came in carrying the martinis. She thought he was smiling at her.

The Meetings

*T*he Whitehall's lounge was small and intimate. The bar would sit only ten people, it was a place where one could spend time and have secretive conversations. Don was meeting Harold Greenberg at six; he was early.

"Hello Mr. Buyers, I haven't seen you in a long time," the bartender immediately said when Don walked in. "Do you want your usual?" Don nodded, and the bartender started to make him a Tanqueray martini, straight up with a lemon twist, just the way he liked them.

Don took the last bar stool with his back against the

wall. "Will there be anyone jointing you this evening?" asked the bartender.

Don nodded again and the bartender put a napkin on the bar next to Don to indicate the seat was taken. Don made some small talk about being in Florida and how he missed the sophistication of Chicago. The bartender agreed, and then left to wait on other people. That gave Don time to ruminate.

Harold Greenberg was one of Chicago's best lawyers and he had the best law firm. He had two offices, one on LaSalle Street and the other in the Evanston. Harold was an extremely honest and loyal attorney. Beneath his Jewish bravado was a moral soul with a strong love for his wife, Goldie and their son, David. That Jew was a contradiction in terms, Don thought. After all, he went to Catholic schools all his life, including Loyola and Notre Dame.

Harold walked in, dispensed with the pleasantries, and ordered a Chivas and water with a twist on the rocks. He reached into his jacket breast pocket and took out four folded sheets of typed paper. "I have most of the information you requested"

"Good," said Don. "What do you have on the Crab Lady's property?"

"Nothing."

"Nothing? How could that be?"

"In the courthouse records there is nothing indicating that she owns any land, especially the parcel you indicated."

"I knew something was strange," Don said. "I purchased all the land west of the road from Turtle Creek

Bridge to the Bay, all the land on the Key, and parcels of land east of the road. That's one reason I called you; she lives on the bay in the middle of land I just bought. But she doesn't own the land. So, is she squatting?"

"Could be, there wasn't anything in the courthouse records. Do you know her name, address, phone number; anything ?"

"She lives in a shack on the water, no electricity, no running water, and no phone," Buyers said. "So, maybe that is why she was so upset last week when we moved some heavy equipment on the Key."

Harold took a sip of his drink and played with his lower lip as he thought about the Crab Lady. "Okay," he said. Here's what we have on that ice cream lady: "Kathryn Callahan, age thirty-seven, widowed at age twenty-eight, married to Hank Callahan, died of lung cancer eight years ago, two boys ages fifteen and fourteen. She is educated, graduated Ohio State University BA with a major in art history, minor in design, comes from a middle class family, no arrests, no driving violations, left a good paying job—she was a buyer for Federated Department stores—to move to Florida two years ago."

"Why did she make that kind of career change?"

"Why don't you ask her that question?" Harold asked.

"I may just do that sometime in the future. Right now, I'd like to get her on board, just to smooth the waters down there. Besides, to build this the way I want, I have to take her business."

Don finished his martini and tapped the top of his

glass. The bartender jumped at the cue.

"Refill, Mr. Greenberg?"

Harold nodded.

"Her oldest son showed me where the cuts are in the mangroves on both sides of the Bay. Jim and I checked them out and we can use them. That kid saved me a fortune because we need a place to offload heavy equipment and supplies. Otherwise I would have to buy or rent an easement or hire a barge for everything. The kid saw a pick-up truck that we found on the island and he wants to make a deal for it."

"So, give him the truck. I guess it's okay to pet the calves to get close to the cow."

With that said, Harold drank his drink in silence.

"What do you have on Jim?

Harold took a deep breath. "Jim Morris, age forty-two, graduated from the University of Georgia, major hydraulic engineering, retired navy seal I think. His records are sealed. He has worked construction up and down Florida and the Southeast.

"He came highly recommended."

"There is one other person you should look out for."

"Really, who's that?"

"When I was snooping around this name came up a few times and I took it upon myself to check him out. There's an ex-heavyweight boxing champion living in your area and he just bought a parcel of land between the Shell Creek Bridge and the Turtle Creek Bridge. Did you know that?"

Don instantly sat up straight; he was half listening to

Harold.

"What the heck is he doing down there?"

"As far as I could find out, he is about to do some developing himself. He has money, not as much as you, but enough. He keeps a low profile. He has a daughter in an expensive private school. He still owns a gym in Brooklyn, he has a manager/partner and he makes frequent trips back and forth. I thought you might want to know. Maybe you two should get together

Don's drummed the bar with his fingers as he pondered the news.

"By the way," Harold asked. "How is my girl, Isabelle?"

"I should have never taken her back. Things are difficult at times." Replied Don.

"So why did you take her back?"

"I felt sorry for her."

"Bullshit, you were horny."

"Harold, I'm not in love with her."

"So? You could send her my way, if you're bored stiff of her. I'll teach her what you didn't. Is she still hot?"

"Yes, she is still hot, but I am not sending her your way." "Didn't the good brothers at Notre Dame and Loyola teach you any better?"

"You're going to deny your friend some fun?"

"No, I am just thinking of Goldie."

"There is no need for you to worry about Goldie, she's in good hands."

They both laughed, then Buyers got down to business. "Harold, I need you to come to Florida I have a lot of things that need to be settled. I bought all the land because it was a good price, and I got the units per acre I wanted on the Key. County rezoned the land for 25 units per acre. That means I can do just about what I want; there are limitations like height, but nothing really limiting. What I need from you is to nail down all the loose ends."

Buyers described how he needed a good, tight survey.

"None of this '500 feet to large palm tree and then north to the large stone, shit,'" he swore. "I also want to own the water rights and the bottomland under the water in certain areas. For instance, I just found that cut in the mangroves is large enough to put in a large boat dock, maybe a small marina or a boat landing to ferry guests back and forth to the Key."

"OK," Harold said. "Sounds good."

"But I need to know if I can put in docks, a marina, a restaurant and more important; if we can fill in marshes," Buyers inquired. "The existing road is half shell and in places asphalt. I want the county to expand the road and replace the bridges and make the expanse higher, which will expand the boating to the east side of the road."

"How soon do you want to move on this?" Harold asked as he took notes.

"Now! There are three or four waterways on the east side of the road and a whole lot of land to be developed," Buyers said. "But we need all the permits in place before the whole world of developers comes down and starts buying parcels. When that happens the county will get wise and start putting sanctions in place. I am first and I want it all. I want to be able to build a boat dock where I see fit. I want permits to fill in swampland and marshes. I want density as high as I find necessary. Those things you can do for me."

"I have a feeling this shopping list isn't finished,"

"That's right, Harold it's not finished." Don went on explaining his dream. "I want you to broker some deals for me. I would be willing to donate the land on the west side and the east side of the road to the county when they widen the road. That would save them a ton of time and money getting easements. I want them to put in a firehouse because no one will spend a million dollars on a house without a fire department. I also want some kind of law enforcement. People like to feel safe. If there is anything I missed you will surely find the loose ends." Harold made some more notes on the back of the sheets of paper he had taken from his pocket; he said nothing for a minute. He finished his scotch and motioned to the bartender.

"What you want, is to broker all these demands before anyone realizes what you're up to. How many years are we talking about?" Harold asked.

"The key alone will take ten years or more to build out; the land along the road, who knows? Maybe another ten years. But if I don't want to finish, or I get bored of Florida I could then sell the parcels. Down the road that land will be worth a fortune, especially if I hold the permits for boat docks, to fill in the land, and permits to cut or trim the mangroves."

Harold nodded "All of this will take some time, I'm

going to have to spend time in Florida. Some of the work I can do from here, but I would like to see the project, especially the Key."

"Harold, I almost forgot, No Wake Zones. I want the county to install markers for no wake zones. People who live on the water don't want fishermen and kids running their boats at top speed pushing wakes on shore over their manicured lawns."

"Okay," Harold raised his glass to Don, and then laughed. "Well, are you trying to out do Tennessee Williams' GLASS MENGERIE? You have a crab lady, an entrepreneur ice cream merchant, a nymphomaniac, a tough-guy hydrologist, Tom Sawyer and Huckleberry Finn. Now, you can add a Jew lawyer who has the blessing of the pope into the mix."

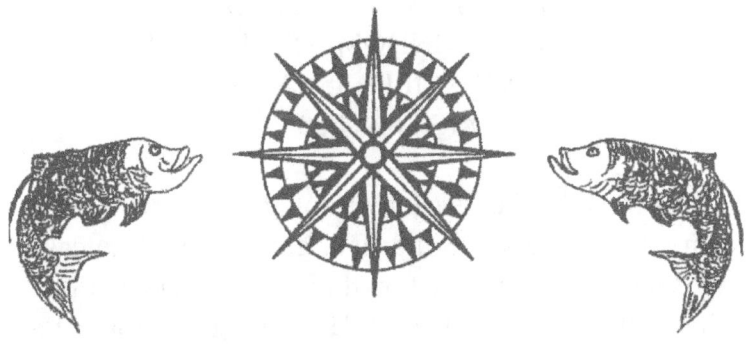

Mmmmm, What a Sweet Morsel

Kate woke up early Thursday morning, fed the boys, and sent them off to school. She stood in front of her closet door deciding what to wear to this meeting. As she looked through her clothes and fixed her eyes on a white suit she hadn't worn since she came to Florida. It was a light wool business suit she wore to executive meetings. She thought this was a business meeting of sorts. County officials will be there, Don Buyers, whom she has not met, and the rest of his entourage. Why not look the part, she thought, so she put on the white suit on with a trendy silk blue blouse and stacked heels. She took a quick look in the mirror, thought she looked quit natty and out the door she went.

Kate drove south down Shell Creek Drive until she came to sign that read:

DON BUYERS LAND DEVELOPMENT
GASPARILLA CONDOMINIUM PROJECT
GASPARILLA ISLAND
813-366-0000

This must be the place, she thought. Kate parked the car in what shade she could find, grabbed her briefcase, and rushed to the construction trailer. There she met Karl Steiner, the project manager. He apologized that Don Buyers would not be here that he had a meeting in Chicago. Karl was a towering man with black curly hair, and the most enormous blue eyes. You could lose yourself in those eyes, Kate thought. But he had a mouth that was soft, fleshy, and weak.

He escorted Kate into the trailer and introduced her as project design manager. Not only was Kate surprised but also she considered the news unsettling. There were several men waiting around drinking coffee and smoking cigarettes. Rather than protest now. She decided she would straighten the design matter latter. The room was rather large and roomy for a construction trailer. One wall had shelves with at least eight Mr. Coffee makers and several coffee warmers. On top of each warmer was a pot of coffee. Kate counted twelve pots of coffee.

Karl introduced Brian, the accountant. He was neatly

dressed in a polo shirt and khaki pants, somehow he looked very familiar. Kate couldn't place him at the moment. He was busy counting the holes in the acoustical ceiling, apparently bored out of his skull. When Kate was introduced, he nodded his head went back to counting holes. There was Gunner, a scary-looking person. His complexion was pasty white; he had sunken gray eyes and a short brush cut. He was the superintendent. The engineer was a very tall man about six foot seven inches and very thin. If he stood sideways he would disappear. His name was Lou. Lou had the shakes. His coffee cup rattled against his saucer. When he used his free hand to steady the cup, all of him shook.

With introductions over Karl, talked about himself and his personal history. He was a developer from California. He had made his money in time-share condominiums. He was one of the first to innovate the idea on the West Coast and then later in Las Vegas. As more developers got into the time-share idea, Karl decided to find new territory. Southwest Florida met the criteria, with plenty of water front property just waiting to be exploited. He rambled on for some time about the manner in which he wanted things handled. He painted a picture of himself as a business mogul well versed in the ways of land development. He laid the groundwork for a smooth running project. At eleven o'clock he stopped abruptly.

"Where is Jim?" he asked. No one answered. Kate looked at Lou, who was sitting next to her, and asked, "Who is Jim?"

"He is the contractor on record," Lou answered. "He is the boss." I nodded as Karl droned on about punctuality and the importance of being on time for our weekly meetings. Suddenly the trailer door opened and in came the most despicable person Kate had ever laid eyes on. In it came. Its smell preceded the creature. Stale booze, cigarette smoke, body order, garlic, grease and the unmistakable odor of old sex wafted across the room. It wore a navy blue T-shirt and wrinkled blue jeans. His clothes were covered with lint and grease marks. He was a big man, at least six foot, maybe more, and weighed about 300 pounds of muscle—no fat. One had to look closely to find a face. Somewhere hidden behind the hair that hung in his eyes and a long shaggy beard, there was a nose and large protruding green eyes.

"Well, Jim, thanks for joining us," Karl said in a sarcastic manner.

"My cow got out," Jim mumbled. "Gunner, get me a cup of coffee."

So, this is Jim, Kate thought, I wonder what kind of cows he had. Kate's family raised cattle back in Ohio. But somehow, she didn't think that's what he meant.

"Are you the designer?" Jim asked Kate.

"No."

He ignored her answer. "When you make the beds in the models, put sheets on them," he nodded his head to emphasis the point. "All you decorators never put sheets on-under those bed spreads."

Kate just looked at him.

"Never mind the sheets, Jim." Karl said. "We have

more important things to discuss."

The conversation went along the lines of technical matters such as trusses, cement, codes, permits, well-points, sub-contractors, land clearing, starting dates, models, projected sales, county codes, and finally moving the construction trailer. Karl left right after the meeting. Kate picked up her briefcase and moved toward the door. Jim stopped her.

"Do you like my boots?"

"I guess they are all right." Kate gave Jim an indifferent look.

"Whaddya mean? These are expensive boots. Gunner. Ain't these expensive boots? Get me another cup of coffee."

"Yeah, boss," Gunner, answered. "Those are expensive boots."

"You betcha, they're expensive boots." Jim repeated himself.

"Okay, I believe you." An exasperated Kate answered

"You want to go on a gator hunt tonight?" Jim asked. "I'll even give you a ride on a Cat. All you Yankee girls like to ride Cats."

"Nope."

"You got any nail polish in that bag?"

"Nail polish? Why would I have nail polish in my briefcase?"

"Because most ladies carry nail polish, you know, in case they get a run in their stockings. You know. But than again you ain't wearing stockings."

"Sorry, no nail polishes."

"Gunner, get nail polish while you're at lunch. Different colors and while you're at it, number the gophers."

"Okay, boss, any special color you want?"

"Yep, pussy pink."

"Okay, boss."

With that conversation still spinning in her mind, Kate left the trailer and went across the street for a quick lunch before heading back to Ice Cream Shop. The restaurant was nondescript and not worthy of the time spent on description. She found a table by the window, sat down, and began processing the meeting. Who is this Karl? Wasn't Don Buyers the headcheese? Everyone seemed like they were out of a comic book, was that a meeting or a joke? Jim had mocked Karl, in fact he mocked everyone, but he had a compelling personality in an abstract way. There had to be serious money behind this project. Her gut feelings told her to get out of Dodge.

Her gloomy train of thought was broken when Jim sat down at her table. "The shrimp Creole is really good. I figured I would join you. You don't mind?" He yelled to the waitress. "We'll have two shrimp Creoles." He sat down, ordered lunch, and begged his pardon all in one breadth.

"I am going to take you out to the project after lunch."

"I thought this was the project"

"No, the project is on Gasparilla Island. We are going to build a model where the trailer is now. The trailer will be moved on site. The model will act as sales office and a place to take the snowbirds. You'll probably stay on the mainland and work with the customers here. All selections of carpet, tiles, and wall paper will be made at the sales office."

"Oh." Kate said. "But what makes you so sure I am going to do this?"

"Because that's what Mr. Buyers wants."

"Really?"

While Jim was talking Kate scrutinized him up close. He had huge forearms with large heart tattoos. In the middle of the tattoos, "Mom" was printed.

"Why not Mary or Sue?" Kate asked.

"What?"

Kate pointed to his arms.

He laughed. "This way no one can ever get mad. Most women become moms sooner or later.

"Looks like a Navy tattoo."

"Does a Navy tattoo look different from an Army tattoo or a Marine tattoo for that matter?"

"No, but I assumed the Navy."

"How did you guess?"

"Because you act like Black Beard, captain of Queen Ann's Revenge."

Jim laughed. The waitress brought the shrimp Creole. Jim was right. It was delicious. I could not believe my eyes; he was picking the shrimp out of the rice and sauce with his fingers. He soon had droppings of tomato sauce and rice interwoven in the red hairs of his beard.

"Do you always use your beard as a napkin?"

"Only when I want to impress people," he said, talking around the food in his mouth.

His left eye seemed to move independently from his right eye. The way he cocked his head, lifted his left brow, and stared at Kate gave her the willies.

Jim suggested they return to the trailer after lunch. Kate started to beg off, but figured she would continue to monitor this fascinating creature.

At the construction trailer, Jim opened the door and Kate went in first. She jumped back in surprise. Large turtles were running all over the floor!

"Gopher turtles?" she asked.

"Gopher turtles," Gunner answered.

"Did you get the right shade of pink for my turtle?" Jim asked.

"See for yourself, boss," Gunner said.

The other men in the construction trailer just ignored Kate. They were too involved painting their gophers. So she just stood there and took at the scene. Against the wall leaning by the coffee pots was a tote board. On the board, listed alphabetically were the names of the gophers and their owners. Next to the names were the odds, next to the odds were bets placed. On the telephone was a young attractive lady. Since she was the only other woman in the trailer, Kate decided to go over and introduce herself. She waved, then extended her hand as the woman continued speaking into the phone.

"Okay, I'll wait, sir," the woman said into the phone. She pushed her chin and shoulder together to cradle the phone, looked up, and shook Kate's hand.

"Hi there, I'm Kate, what's all the fuss about?"

"Is there enough testosterone in here or what?" she said with a wry grin. "Hi, I'm Isabelle."

Kate motioned to the phone. "Don't you…?"

"Oh, God, no," Isabelle replied. "It's just another guy wanting to enter his turtle. He's checking to see if it's the minimum size—oh, that's right, sir, and your turtle does measure up. See you at the races." She hung up the phone.

"Turtle?" Kate asked.

"You don't know about the races?" Isabelle asked.

Kate shook her head.

"Come on," Isabelle said, "I can use a smoke. Let's get out of this man cave and I'll tell you all about it."

As they talked, Kate was impressed with the poise and beauty of her new friend. Isabelle seemed to be a slice of big city glamour plunked down in the middle of nowhere. Her excitement was infectious; Kate couldn't stop laughing as Isabelle described the preparations for the gopher turtle race.

"Lou was painting his gopher with white nail polish and sprinkling silver glitter on the wet polish," Isabelle said. "One gopher has a yellow ribbon glued to its back because Brian is from Texas. And Gunner's gopher is painted sort of like, psychedelic, with some sort of geometric pattern in purple and orange."

Isabelle explained that she was Don Buyers' assistant, and that he had flown her down to organize things in his field office. As she talked, Kate noticed an undercurrent of tension, as if Isabelle, despite her beauty and make-up, had some issues that perhaps she didn't even know about. Kate looked into one of the big windows of the trailer. Several gophers were in cages waiting for their owners. A steady stream of construction workers came past. They ogled the two women before entering the trailer to grab some coffee, pick a turtle, and paint it.

"Imagine a group of grown men giggling and hooting and slapping their legs and stumping their feet like that," Kate whispered as the two women re-entered the trailer. Every time someone slapped his legs a cloud of dust rose into the atmosphere. Isabelle, who wore high heels, had to step carefully. There were gophers everywhere trying to hide under chairs, behind the sofa, and under papers. One even tried to burrow a hole under the rug. Men kept coming and going.

"Why don't you all come back this evening for the gopher race, bring your boys." Gunner asked Kate.

"My boys?"

"Yeah, both of the boys. They've been sniffing around here looking for jobs."

Before Kate could respond Jim roared out of an inner office of the trailer like a dervish. He was anxious to show Kate the property before the tide changed.

"I'll see you tonight?" Isabelle called out from her desk.

"I'll be there," Kate said, surprised that she had agreed so readily.

"We'll take my Jeep." Jim said. In contrast to Jim's appearance the Jeep was surprisingly clean. The close quarters of the Jeep made his odoriferous smell unbearable, so Kate quickly rolled down a window. Just stay up wind, she thought.

They drove to the inlet where his boat was moored. It was a small shallow-draft boat with the motor in the center between the stern and the bow. Kate didn't recognize the style. A girl of the Midwest, she had never seen a boat like it on Lake Michigan or Lake Erie for that matter. She discovered later it was designed for mullet fishing.

"We're going by boat?" Kate asked.

"No, we're gonna walk across the water," Jim said. "Oh, I forgot, only one of us can do that!"

Smartass, Kate thought as she clambered into the vessel.

She sat on an overturned five-gallon bucket; Jim put the boat on plane and off they went. The wind and the occasional spray of water made Kate shiver even though she was wearing a wool jacket. She kept watching the shoreline and making mental markers on the variation in the land just in case she returned without Jim; Kate trusted him but he was one strange dude. They flew across the Bay in minutes, and then Jim left the waterway.

As he zipped between small mangrove islands, Kate began to lose her bearings. Jim took what seemed like a zigzag course between islands until Kate lost site of the inlet. He slowed down almost to idle speed then crept to what looked like land at the end of the basin. When the boat reached the other side Jim turned off the motor, pulled up the prop, and began to pole his way into the mangroves.

As the bow of the boat went under branches of buttonwood mangroves, Jim took his machete and chopped the lower limbs. Kate ducked. The boat barely slid through the narrow cut that was five to six feet wide.

"How deep is the water?" Kate asked.

"Maybe, six inches, that's why I wanted to get here during high tide, or we would never get through otherwise."

As the boat slipped through the cut, the mangroves closed in behind them. Kate felt swallowed alive in some obscured place in the Amazon Jungle.

They finally emerged into a large lagoon. Kate couldn't believe her eyes, the scene before her was one of beauty and tranquility? White Ibises were perched in the mangroves, which reflected a mirror image in the water. It was unbelievably beautiful, primitive, and pristine. The only sound was Jim poling the boat through the water. Across the lagoon was an old dock that looked sturdy enough. As the boat entered deeper water, Jim put the motor down, cranked up the engine, and made for the dock.

"Where did the dock come from? Certainly no Indians built that."

"Probably some pirates, who came here to hide their loot, or maybe they captured fair-haired maidens to rape." As Jim answered his left eye twinkled. She sized up the situation as Jim laid anchor and secured the boat. No one would ever find me here, she thought.

The dock protruded into the water about twenty feet. On the port side there was approximately a hundred yards of swamp. Growing out of the ground were thousands of sticks or what seemed to be sticks ranging in size from three to six inches. Previous visitors had made a makeshift walk over part of the swamp with planking, but it went only part way.

Jim handed her a pair of rubber boots.

"You'd better put these on. They're probably too big, but you'll need them to get across the mud."

Kate took off her shoes and put her feet into the oversized boots; they were so big she could hardly walk. When they reached the end of the planks, Jim got in front of her.

"I'm going to give you your first lesson in traversing a swamp. See, those mangrove fingers? Step on them and you won't sink up to your armpits or, would you prefer I carry you."

"No, I am a quick learner."

"Follow me."

He stepped off the planks took several steps. It looked easy enough. He stopped. "Your turn. Be careful, just think what you may have to give me if, I have to pull you out." He chuckled.

"Put your lustful mind at ease," Kate snapped. "You won't have the opportunity."

She took her first step, no problem; she took a second, piece of cake. Kate got her confidence back, took a third, and then a forth. But then a breeze came up. She was downwind and almost gagged. She lost her footing, slipped off the mangrove shoot, and found her right leg buried in the muck up to her knee. She reached down to steady herself and her arm was in the Florida muck up to her elbow.

Jim came back and pulled Kate out. She was covered in mud. Suddenly the chic white suit wasn't very chic, or very white.

"Do you want to go back?"

"It is a little late for going back," she answered gamely. "Let's keep going."

Beyond the swamp was a very faint trail that wound around an old Indian shell mound. They started up a gradual grade that began to get steeper. Kate reached a point where she could no longer walk in the over-sized boots,

"Jim, I'm going to take them off and walk barefoot."

"Go ahead, I'll wait."

She stepped out of the boots.

Moments later, Jim stopped and grinned. "You must be a sweet morsel, Mmmmm-Mmmmmm." He looked at her feet and his stare slowly advanced up her whole body. Then he licked his lips, as though he just finished eating a cream puff. Kate blushed and glared back. Then he pointed to her feet.

Kate looked down and saw a hundred fire ants crawling on her feet and legs. Just as she began to swat them they gave the signal to bite. Soon Kate was jumping, swinging, and hitting, all at the same time. There is nothing as torturous as the bite from a fire ant.

"And, you thought I meant you were sweet." Jim

laughed. "I was speaking for the ants!"

He daubed mud on Kate's feet and legs, smothering the critters, the pain, and the last vestiges of elegance the white suit had once possessed.

Kate raced him to the summit, eager to escape the ant world. At the summit of the mound, about thirty feet above sea level, they encountered a panoramic view of the Gulf shoreline and the mangrove coastline. Jim pointed out details: over there will be a twenty-seven-hole golf course, there a swimming pool, there the tennis courts and there will be the condominiums.

The land would be divided into sections, residential homes and villas surrounding the golf course. The condominiums would flank the pool, clubhouse, and tennis courts. The pristine lagoon will be made into a small marina for the residents with a small restaurant and a tike bar.

Somewhere during Jim's speech Kate stopped listening and started looking. This was one of the most beautiful pieces of land I have ever seen, she thought as he droned on. Look at that long stretch of beach with amazing white sand, with sea oats and flowering sea grapes. The land was wild and free. As she turned and looked south across the bay the Crab Lady's boat dock came into view as it stretched into the bay.

"Does anyone live here?"

"Once; there are a few abandoned shacks but nothing else."

"What are you going to do with the swamp?'

"Drain it, fill it, and put in a retention lake."

"What about the mangroves on the bay side?'

"Pull them out, put in boat docks and short canals with homes on both sides.

"What about this shell mound, we are standing on? Doesn't it have some historical significance?

"Level it."

"This land isn't that wide; you can see both bay and Gulf."

"It is deceiving," Jim said. "It's long and narrow. You would be surprised how many units we can get out of this piece of land."

"How many units?"

"Maybe, fifty, say sixty per acre."

"You can't do this," Kate blurted out. "It would be a rape. You would destroy this beauty? Once it is gone, you can never, never replace it. Why trade this for concrete and fifty units an acre? What a travesty.

"If we don't, someone else will."

"You can't destroy this."

"The land has been bought and paid for, permits have been approved. The die has been cast."

Kate walked down to the beach. It was bare except for a few broken-down cottages. The beach was void of all human life. Along the shoreline a string of blue crabs ran in single file. I never saw this before, she thought, and probably never will again. They sparkled in the sun light, their blue shells luminescent in the glare. Kate walked along thinking about the unusual day and how so much of what she saw would soon be gone.

Jim, who had been checking surveyor's stakes,

bellowed. "Hey, wake up. We have to get out of here before the tide changes."

Kate barely said ten words all the way back to the construction trailer. Her suit, once as bright and pristine as the secret beach she had just discovered, was ruined. But that loss barely registered. She thought of that beach; she felt like a mourner who had come too soon. The victim still lived, but she could see its end laid out before her. Jim sensed her mood, and by some great effort turned his energy way down low.

She got out of the jeep, closed the door, and looked back.

"Good-bye, Jim," She said.

He trained one eye on her, and then shrugged his shoulders. "Change happens."

Back home Kate took a shower. She then put on a pair of old blue jeans and a sweatshirt. She found a plastic bag in the closet, stuffed the white suit in it, and threw it in the trash.

Don Pedro Island - 1979

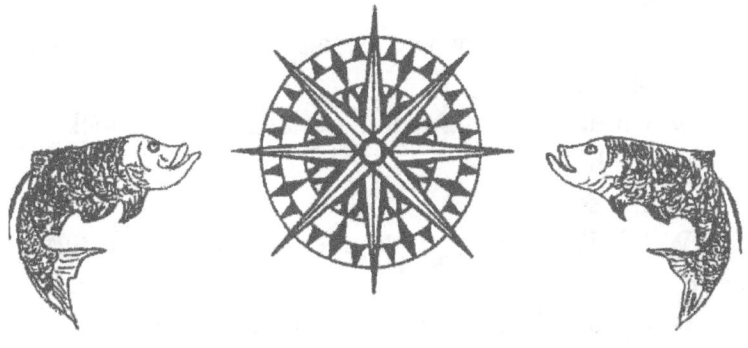

The Gopher Turtle Races

*K*ate was making super when the boys came home excited.

"Mom, there's going to be a gopher turtle race this evening, " Steven shouted by way of greeting. "Can we go?"

"How did you know that?"

"Everyone at school was talking about it," he said. "All the kids I know are going, we want to go, please.

"I just started cooking."

"Don't worry about it. They have food there." Steve

countered. "We've never seen a turtle race, have you?"

She thought about that for a minute. He was right, Kate thought. I've never seen a turtle race. And, Gunner did invite me this afternoon. I did see all those turtles running around that construction trailer. Why not, I could use a change of attitude.

"What time and where is this event going to take place?" she asked

"Down at the construction site about six o'clock. Is that right, Phil?"

"I think so."

"Well," Kate said. "What does one wear to a turtle race?"

"Blue jeans." Both boys said simultaneously.

"Okay, go get cleaned up and we'll go."

As she drove down the road to the construction site Kate noticed there were cars parked on both sides of the road. The parking lot around the trailer was stuffed with cars and trucks crammed in precarious angles in that small space.

Across the street, Brian was supervising the parking of cars in a field. He recognized Kate and flagged her over. "Hi Kate, glad you could come. It should be a lotta fun tonight. Go ahead and park next to that yellow pick-up. See you later." He went back to directing the line of cars behind her.

Kate was astonished that there were so many people in attendance. She didn't know Shell Creek had that many residents. I thought I knew everyone, but I guess I was wrong, she thought, chastened. There were so many unfamiliar faces and, to her surprise, lots and lots of children between the ages of five and eighteen. She looked for the Crab Lady, but she and her family were not present. Roger waved her over. He was with his wife and two of the fishermen that come into the into the ice cream shop for coffee, Chappie and his new girlfriend, and Harold. At that moment her two boys decided to take leave of Kate.

"Mom, we are going to check things out, okay." Phil said.

"Okay"

Roger introduced Kate to his wife. They exchanged greetings as Brian entered the little group. "This is one hell of a party," Roger said. "Is Don Buyers going to be here?"

"No. He is still in Chicago working out some legal details," Brian answered. "He doesn't know about this party, I expect he won't be too happy when he finds out."

What do you mean?" Chappie asked.

"It was Big Jim's idea," Brian said. "He believes you start a project with a party and when the first building is topped out, we have a huge bash."

"I like that idea." Ellen spoke up. She was Harold's wife.

"When is Don Buyers coming back?" Roger inquired.

"The first of next week."

"I've never met him." Kate said.

"Yes, you have." Brian stated emphatically.

"No, I don't think so."

"Let me refresh your memory," he said. "We were in your ice cream shop; let me think, not quite a year ago. There were four of us on a tarpon-fishing trip and we came looking for the Crab Lady. Now do you remember?"

"Oh, how well I do," Kate, said. She instinctively looked at his shirt to see what logo he was wearing. If I remember right he had on a yellow shirt and a green penguin, she thought, so which one was Don Buyers? The answer came like a flash of lightning. "The alligator."

"What did you say?"

"Nothing, I have so many people that come into the shop, it is impossible to recognize everyone. So, you work for Don Buyers. In what capacity and did you have to move here?"

Carrie, a stylish woman Brian had introduced as his wife, spoke up. "We moved here a few a weeks ago and I hate it here. This has to be the end of the world; Timbuktu would offer more excitement."

"Speaking of excitement, when was the last time you were invited to a gopher race, Miss Carrie?" Big Jim had just sauntered into the conversation. What an improvement over this morning, Kate thought. There was no trailing or preceding odor, he had a haircut, and his beard was trim. He wore a clean, pressed, green khaki shirt, blue jeans, and of course his new cowboy boots.

"If you wait long enough, I am sure there will be a Sak's Fifth Avenue," Kate said. Seeing Jim reminded her of the death sentence he was executing on the pristine beach and unspoiled hammocks she had seen earlier that day. "When they finally complete the building project on the key you can become a member of the country club and play golf every day."

"Now, Kate, you be kind." Roger spoke. "We all know how you hate progress, but just think of the employment that means for the people down here, like the carpenters, electricians, plumbers, painters, bricklayers, cement people, landscapers…"

"I gotta admit, he's got a point," Chappie chimed in. "Why, right now the only way you can make money around here is by fishin' or smugglin', an' I'm too old to be cattin' around at night."

"Honey you forgot to mention tarpon fishing." Chappie's girlfriend gave Kate a look that could kill.

"Yeah, she will kick your ass if you're out after nine." Roger crowed. "But think about it, if you add the Bay side property and once the bridges are replaced we'll be busy for the next twenty years or more. I won't have to worry how I am going to afford to send my son to college."

"I understand," Kate countered. "But when you think of all those new people... What is the average person per household 2.1 or is it 2.5, whatever the number, times that by what, 1,000 new households? Maybe 2,000?" Kate looked at Big Jim, who shrugged his shoulders. "Are we prepared to handle 25,000 to 50,000 new residents here? When was the last time you had a speeding ticket?"

Roger shook his head back and forth. "Never."

"Well that will stop. As soon as the first condo is sold we'll have a police force, and fire department, and then a hospital; which is not a bad thing. Then come the shopping malls, and all the benefits that follow prosperity. Traffic lights, street lights, four lane highways, schools, doctors, dentist, lawyers, bankers, crime, and all the things we came here to get away from."

"Well Kate I hope Sak's gets here in a hurry." Carrie moaned.

"Remind me not to invite you to my next party, Ms. Wet Blanket," Jim growled at Kate. Turning his back on her, he spread his arms wide and in a booming voice called out, "Come on, let's get a bite to eat, it is all Florida Cracker delicacies." He led the way to the food table and the group around Kate all followed.

There was more food than you would find at an Italian wedding, Kate thought, and I'm Italian so I should know. The gigantic table extended at least 50 feet in length. People started to queue up. Jim nonchalantly stepped in front of the line like he was expected to lead.

There were raw oysters, barbeque oysters, swamp cabbage, smoked mullet, barbeque mullet, corn on the cob, fried okra, smoked grouper, fried gator tail, and shrimp.

Not to mention deviled crabs, sliced tomatoes, mangoes, avocados and clam chowder made from bay clams. There was ice tea, lemonade, coffee, and a keg of beer and for dessert they offered apple pie, pecan pie, lemon marangue pie, key lime pie, sweet potato pie, chocolate devil food cake, brownies, peanut butter cookies and vanilla ice cream from the local grocery store.

"What is swamp cabbage?" Kate asked Chappie.

Before he could answer, one of Kate's sons came running up. "Mom, you have any money? Lilly Langtry has odds of five to one. If I bet one dollar that means I get five dollars back."

"Philip, I know what five to one means."

"Mom, she is running in the next race, if she wins I'll pay you back the dollar."

"Where is your bother?"

"Over there talking to Roger." Phil pointed in the direction of Roger.

"Phil will you eat something?"

"Yeah, after the next race."

She reached into her pants pocket and extracted two dollars; Kate gave one to Phil and told him to give his brother the other one. "And don't forget to pay me back if you win!" Phil took off.

Suddenly Big Jim loomed before Kate, holding two plates heaped with what appeared to be everything from the serving table. "You were asking about swamp cabbage?" He had a wise owl look on his face as he led her to a table. "Have you ever had hearts of palm on your salad in those fancy northern restaurants?"

"Yes, but hearts of palm are not from Florida."

"You don't think so? What are those trees over there called?"

He was delighted in goading Kate.

She followed his pointed finger. "Those are palm trees." She smarted back at him.

"Yeah, but what kind of palm tree?"

Kate just glared at him; where is he going with this? She thought.

"Let me inform you that those are called cabbage palm trees, and rightfully so because the heart of those palms is what you Yankees call 'hearts of palm' and we red-necks get swamp cabbage from them."

"How do you extract the heart out of the palm tree?"

"Difficult and time consuming I'll show how someday."

"Mom, the race is going to begin," Phil said. "Let's see if Lilly Langtry will win"

Across the patch of grass where the tables had been set up, a crowd gathered near a cordoned-off stretch of turf. Below them, the small gopher turtles started the first of a series of heats, punctuated by drinking and shouting.

The races ran in intervals. There were thirty-two gopher turtles in all and eight mini-races of four gophers each. The winners of each of small races competed in the final heat for the title of King Gopher or Queen Gopher. Twenty minutes separated the mini races; this allowed everyone a chance to refill their beers or get a bite to eat. Several races were run before Kate arrived and three events remained before the finals. Each participant had his or her own turtle in a separate cage or box and each turtle is clearly identified with either a name or number. After the race was over the turtles were turned back into the wild.

The "racetrack" was approximately 20 feet long and eight feet wide. Two by six boards lay around the perimeter and two by fours divided each lane to keep the turtles in their lanes. As Kate's small entourage walked towards the racetrack, she could almost feel the excitement. By the back door of the construction trailer a few men were setting up a bandstand. The musicians were in the middle of running electricity from the trailer to the speakers and amplifiers.

Isabelle was as beautiful as ever as she hustled around supervising both the race and the music. She wore skintight blue jeans, a white camp blouse with the top three buttons left undone revealing tantalizing cleavage, and what appeared to be the most expensive cowboy boots that Don Buyers could buy. To Kate, she looked like a cross between Jean Harlow and Daisy Mae, sophistication and country. Every male, including Kate's teenage boys, ogled her.

Roger and Jim appeared to be the only men unaffected by her beauty. Roger was so into his wife he never looked further then her face. And, Jim, he treated Isabelle as if she didn't exist. She simply was invisible. She handed him a tout sheet, which he passed to Kate.

Kate laughed at the handicap sheet; it certainly was tongue in cheek. The gophers were contained in their cages or boxes until race time. Children huddled around the cages trying to pet them and look at the designs on their back.

The band gave a fanfare and Isabelle announced the

The beginning of the final three races. She gave the turtles names, "Lily Langtry, Judge Roy Beane, Spiderman, and Mao, would you please take your place at the starting line. When you hear the sound of the gun, the race will begin.

People crowded around the track

"Bang"

"Folks, they are off and running," Lou shouted. "Lily has a head start; no, here comes the Judge. Wait a minute folks, Mao has changed his mind. He turned around and is retreating. Spiderman can't figure out what to do. He is just standing there. But, here comes the Judge. He is catching up to Miss Lilly—wait a minute; folks, Spiderman is on all fours! He looks like he found his web. Lilly is close to the finish line. Where is the Judge? Oh! My! Look, at Spiderman. He is making his move; he is up and look at him run! I have never seen a gopher turtle run that fast, folks he is on all four little legs and he is going, going, going, and he is gone!

Cheers went up from the crowd.

Spiderman took the race beating Miss Lily Langtry by seconds. Folks, I tell you this was the most exciting race I have seen. When Spiderman raised himself up on all fours there was nothing holding him back. I just have

TOTE BOARD

Lily Langtry	Can she stay ahead of Judge Roy Bean?
Judge Roy Bean	Will Miss Langtry get away from him?
Mao	Can he stay ahead of the Red Army?
Spider Man	Can he run without his web?
Alfalfa	Can he stay ahead of the rascals?
Candy man	Sweet to the last mile.
Tarzan	He is swinging after Jane.
Lone Ranger	Faster then a silver bullet.
Pussy Cat	Pussycat, Pussycat, meow, meow.
Popeye	Did he eat his spinach today?

to say, you can not beat a super hero."

Amid the raucous, laughter, and cries of "fixed," or "the race was rigged," everyone adjourned for more food and alcohol. The band swung into a series of country foot-stomping dance music.

"There will be a twenty-minute break between this race and the next, enjoy an ice-cold beer, and there is plenty of time to stop by the food table," Lou shouted. "Folks, all the food that you are eating has been locally grown or comes from our beautiful Gulf of Mexico."

Phil came back and gave Kate her dollar.

"I thought you placed a bet on Lily Langtry?"

"At the last minute I changed my mind," he said.

"Good for you."

Soon everyone danced; they danced alone, with the kids and in line as they pounded out the Texas Two-Step. The crowd drank more, partying, eating, and drinking until the wee hours of the morning.

Kate made her way home, humming a tune even as her head swirled with the rush of events of the day. First there had been the meeting at the construction trailer, then revelatory boat trip across the bay to the preview of the construction site. She had to admit, however, that the gopher turtle race was the best of times. It created a sense of community that had seemed to be on the back burner. People cared about one another, but there seldom were gatherings where that community spirit was on display.

But even that fun came at a price. She frowned when she considered who had sponsored the event, and the price Shell Creek would have to pay.

The Clash

*D*on Buyers rose early. The sun was just beginning to peak in the east. It was Monday and he was anxious. He felt the world was waiting for him to do something great. He was the man that made a difference; he was on the verge of creating a whole new universe. In his mind's eye he saw the future. He pictured the Key as it would look when the construction and the development was finished. He imagined the beautiful island with Key West architecture against the blue-green Gulf of Mexico, white sand beaches, flowering bougainvillea, coconut palms and colorful hibiscus. He pictured the marina, the boat docks, the tiki bar, the health club, the golf course, and the swimming pools with their Jacuzzis.

"Today we start the construction with the ground-breaking on the Key," he said, speaking a mantra of growth as he made his way to the trailer. "There will be no ceremony, not today. I'll wait till we finish the first phase when the first two holes of the golf course are finished with the swimming pools." He smiled. "That will be enough splendor to make the visitors drool.

It was six a.m. when he arrived at the trailer. He welcomed the fact that he would be alone for at least an hour. The solitude would allow him time to ruminate over the project and go over some paperwork before anyone intruded and the phones began to ring. But his vision of solitary industry was disturbed when he arrived to find Jim's jeep parked next to the construction trailer.

"He's up early," Don mumbled.

He noticed more than two-dozen trash bags piled up against the side of the trailer. When he entered the trailer, Jim was not in his office and the coffee pots were not cleaned. Strange, he thought, Isabelle's a neat freak. On the shelf above her desk was a small wire cage with a turtle inside. It wore a yellow ribbon. Hanging on the cage was a paper sign that read "Miss Lily Langtry."

What the hell is a turtle doing in here? He thought. Don settled behind his desk, retrieved some notes from his attaché case, and began reviewing the notations that Harold had jotted down at the Whitehall. Suddenly the door opened and Isabelle entered, dressed as if she were about to stroll down Fifth Avenue.

He glanced at his watch: it was six fifteen. "You're early."

Isabelle jumped. "You startled me."

"I am sorry, how are you?" Don answered. "What's going on? I see we have a new employee named Miss Lilly Langtry?"

"Oh, she belongs to Gunner," Isabelle said with a laugh. "He forgot to set her loose after the turtle race the other night; I mean the gopher turtle race, you missed it. What a lot of fun we had."

"Pardon me, but what did I miss? Please start from the beginning."

"Well, we had a gopher turtle race last Friday night. Everyone was here, the whole town came; all the kids came with their parents, even the country commissioners and their families. I didn't know so many people lived in Shell Creek." Her eyes glittered with excitement as she relived the events of the past evening. "You should have seen the food! There was swamp cabbage, gator tail, smoked mullet, smoked grouper, all kinds shrimp and crab, and then everyone brought some kind of dessert. We had a band and we danced 'til…" She bit her lip and cut short her breathless narrative as she noticed the expression on Buyers' face.

"Who authorized this shindig?"

"Um, Jim told me to put together a party for everyone involved before we 'break ground', as sort of a kick off. We had so much fun."

"Who paid for all food and who paid for the band?"

"I took the money from petty cash. Most of the food people brought, except the kegs of beer and some miscellaneous things."

"You paid for the beer and the band out of petty cash?" Don asked. His expansive mood of the morning was gone. "What the hell were you thinking? I suppose you organized the gopher race too?"

"Yes, I did, and I did a damn good job," Isabelle snapped. Her face red with rage, she turned her back on Buyers and moved toward the office door.

"Tell Jim I want to see him." Don yelled as she slammed the door behind her.

Don now was so livid he couldn't concentrate on his work. Instead he walked to the window. What he was witnessing surprised him even more. Seven a.m. was still a few minutes away, but the whole crew was busy at work. Brian was motioning everyone to park in the field across the street. Roger and his crew were beginning to erect a chain-link fence to cordon off a parcel of land when a truck pulled up with a load of cement blocks and behind that was a truck carrying trusses. Roger gave his men instructions and gave the truck drivers directions.

Isabelle came back into the office, cleaned up the coffee area, and began brewing pots of coffee for Roger and his crew.

Don glanced at his watch again. His universe had started without him. I haven't been gone a week, he thought, and I have lost control.

A short distance away but in a universe all his own,

The Price of Crabs

Jim walked along the high-tide line of the beach. The only souls he encountered were the sandpipers scurrying across the white sand. He paused a moment and watched the birds play dodgem with the rippling waves. He was there to check on the surveyor's stakes. Today the earth moving would begin.

Jim knew the stakes did not need checking, but something else pulled at his psyche as he walked up the old Indian Shell Mound. Once on top he felt the sea breeze wrap around him and a little chill crawled down his back. He looked across the bay and down to the Crab Lady's boat dock and across the island to the Gulf. As he surveyed the land and water he thought about Kate and her reaction to the plans to transform the community. Sure, sooner or later a developer would do same thing as Don planned—or even worse. At least Buyers had the money and backing to create an aesthetic project; once the word got out, Jim thought, everyone will want to own a piece of this tranquility and they will pay big bucks.

With the toe of his boot he dug in the sand, dirt, and shells under his feet. He reached down and picked up four pieces of pottery shards. He put them in his pocket. Jim looked down around the shell mound. Maybe…

He walked to the water's edge, pulled out one of the shards, and flicked his wrist to send it skipping across the sparkling water of the Gulf. He thought again of Kate. A smile creased Jim's face and his green eyes danced with mischief. Time to get to work, he thought.

Jim scratched on Don's office door. "You wanted to see me?"

Don looked up from his desk. He rose, crossed the office, and stood face to face with Jim. "Who do you think you are? What gave you the right to throw a party last week without consulting with me?"

The two men stood staring at each other marking their territory, both well over six feet tall. Don was lean, tall, and handsome with sophistication that money and breeding impart. Jim was an old salt, with hair like fire, as unruly and ornery as the Scots and Vikings whose renegade blood coursed through his veins. And if Don was angry, Jim's raider blood was up.

"Look, I'm the one who will bring this project to fruition," Jim growled, standing toe to toe with his boss. "I'm the one who will cajole the men to keep working when it's ninety degrees and the humidity is ninety-percent and there is no breeze, sweat pouring down their faces and the no-see-ums and mosquitoes are picking at their flesh. I'm the one who'll have to make 'em lay block faster because a cement truck is waiting to do a pour. Maybe the only thing that'll keep 'em going then is the promise of another party to celebrate the completion of a building."

Don glared at Jim. Damn, he thought, I wish I hadn't started this argument because this smelly redneck is right. But he couldn't say that.

"It is my project and it will be done my way," he snarled.

Jim's lower lip curled. "Don, you do what you do

best, I'll do what I do best." For a moment they both faced each other, cold blue eyes and piercing green eyes locked in a stalemate.

Jim spoke first. "Now, do you have the blueprints ready for the Captiva home that we'll be using for a model?" Don turned and grabbed the blueprints from his desk.

Jim walked to the open window and called for Roger to come into the office. When Roger appeared, the three men discussed the location for building a second model. Soon the tension was dissipated as the three men got down to business.

As Jim was on his way out he turned and mentioned to Don that the barge would arrive at noon and the construction trailer should be packed and ready to move.

"They charge by the hour and I know you don't want to spend an extra dime."

"Okay, okay," Don said. As if it were an afterthought he added, "Jim, did you talk to Kate about coming to work for us?"

"She said she would rather dip ice cream at fifty cents a cone than make lots of money working on a project she doesn't believe in," Jim answered. "Oh, by the way, Don, Isabelle did a fantastic job organizing the gopher turtle race, you might consider an increase in her salary." With that said, Jim walked out.

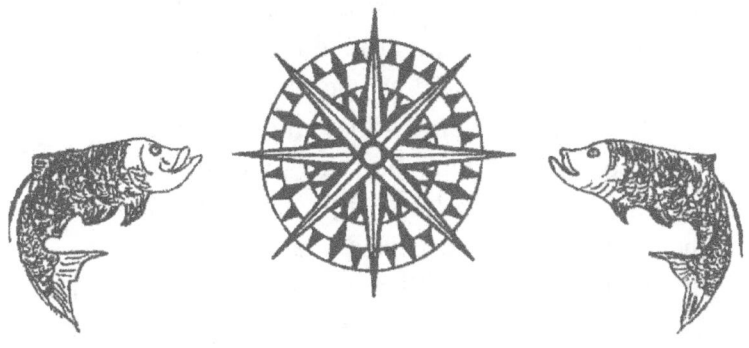

Dali, and the Silvery Moon

s Kate leaned half her body into the coolers cleaning and restocking the ice cream she whined, "I hate Mondays". I hate this chore, she thought, as her hands grew numb. The jingle of the bells on the front door interrupted her complaining.

"Hi, lady."

Kate recognized Jerry's voice.

"Where've you been?"

"Up north."

"Where up north?" Kate asked.

"Brooklyn, checking things out."

"You missed a great party."

"So I heard. They say you're some dancer."

"News travels fast." Kate groaned with chagrin as flickering images of her drunken moonlight dance flashed through her head.

"What did you expect?" he joked. "What happens here is like the bullet heard around the world."

"Whatever," Kate said as she put a cup of coffee in front of Jerry. "I'll remember that bit of wisdom."

The door opened again and this time Isabelle walked in, wearing a multi-colored silk floral sundress with spaghetti straps and high-heeled strapped sandals.

Suddenly Kate felt like a slattern. What woman wouldn't standing next to Isabelle? She is the most striking good-looking woman I have ever seen since I moved to this small nondescript town, Kate thought. How does she do it? Never a hair out of place, perfect make up, clothes always fit perfect like she walked out of Vogue. She looks better in a sweat suit and sneakers then most people do in formal wear.

Jerry choked on his coffee. Kate turned away from Isabelle, asked, "are you alright?" He nodded, yes, trying to recover from the choke. But, Kate noticed he is white as a ghost and with a terrified expression on his face.

"Hi Kate, the boss decided to buy lunch for the gang today," Isabelle crowed.

"You did a great job Friday night, Isabelle," Kate said. "I surprised myself and enjoyed the gopher turtle races and the dancing."

"Especially the dancing," Jerry chimed in.

Kate shot him a look.

"Well, if you heard Don this morning you would have thought I had burned down the farm," Isabelle pouted. "He can be a real bastard at times."

"Then leave his ass," Jerry blurted out.

"Pardon me, but do I know you?"

Isabelle blushed. Damn, Kate thought, even her blushes are attractive. Apparently, Jerry thought the same thing. His gaze was fixed on Isabelle; he stared at her, Kate thought, the way the Crab Lady's retarded boy stared at ice cream.

Isabelle caught his stare; Jerry immediately dropped his head and fumbled in his pockets.

"Uh, Kate, warm up my coffee, wouldya?" he said. "I'm going outside to have a smoke." He turned and left.

Isabelle stared after him for a moment then, flustered, launched into her order.

"I'd like twenty ham and cheese sandwiches, the same number of bags of chips, and a case each of pop and iced tea."

"And to what army am I delivering this order?" Kate asked, hoping to break the tension.

They both laughed, then Isabelle sighed and dropped into one of the wrought-iron chairs.

"Who would have thought that a year ago that I would be living here, Kate?"

"Tell me about it," Kate replied. "Who would have thought I would be living in this small village on Shell Creek."

Isabelle pursed her lips, as if in thought. Suddenly she stood up. "Give me that guy's coffee, I think I'll have a smoke with him, while you make up the sandwiches."

"Do you have an extra cigarette?" Isabelle asked.

Jerry smiled and reached in his shirt pocket for a pack of filtered Camels. He offered her one. "I should quit one of these days."

Isabelle murmured. "I have been told that several times a day."

"My name is Jerry."

"I am Isabelle."

"I'm not good with accents," she said. "How did you find your way to Shell Creek?"

"I'm good with sizing people up," Jerry replied. "How'd a stylish Brooklyn glamour girl like you wind up down here?"

"It's a long story. What did you mean when you said, 'Leave'?"

Jerry curled his lips into a lopsided smile, "I meant leave him."

"Who?"

"The man who's keeping you."

"What do you mean the man who is keeping me?" she said.

"Well, miss, I assume it is miss, anyone who walks into an ice cream shop at ten in the morning; in this neck of the woods looking as well put together as you, surely you are not working construction or cleaning houses or clerking at a local grocery store. This is a backward Florida town in the middle of a swamp with acres of mangroves. The only person you're going to impress is the alligators or maybe a sleepy pelican, or maybe the guy who's keeping you."

"I... I," Isabelle started to say something when Jerry cut her off.

"Look, I am sorry, I spent my whole life judging my opponents, finding their vulnerability, then homing in," Jerry said. "Now I'm beating on a girl. I must be punch-drunk or something. I didn't mean anything." He waved his hand in an apologetic motion and left.

Isabelle stood looking after him. She ground out her cigarette under her brand new heels and walked back into the ice cream shop.

"Who the hell does he think he is?"

"Who, Jerry?"

"Yes, he is the most arrogant man I have ever met."

"You mean Jerry?" Kate asked. "I kind of like him. I even like his ugliness, He is the most down-to-earth person I have met since I came down here to live."

"What do you know about him?"

"Nothing much," Kate replied. "I know he has a business in Brooklyn, that someone manages the place while he is down here. I know he is kind, polite, philosophical, can carry on a good conversation and I guess that is enough for me. I like him, he is a good guy."

"That is where I have seen him, hanging out a window in Brooklyn,"

Isabelle abruptly changed the subject. "Is my order ready?"

"Almost," Kate said. "Give me about ten more minutes, okay?"

She worked fast because she felt that Isabelle was no longer in the mood for small talk. What did Jerry say to her? Kate wondered. One thing she noticed, Jerry seemed to have fallen head over heels for Miss Glamor Girl. Then it appeared that he dug his own grave with his big mouth. But Kate had her own fish to fry, so she just went back to work. Soon she had the order ready. She rang up the bill, Isabelle paid, and Kate helped carry everything to Isabelle's car.

"Thank you." Isabelle said and drove off.

She knew she should have been more gracious, but really! Who was that guy to insult me like that, she fumed silently. He implied that I am a kept woman. How insulting. He made me feel naked, exposed, and I don't like the feeling in the least.

When she arrived at the construction trailer, Gunner came out and helped her unpack the car and set up the food in the parking area. The men were hungry and they chowed down as if they had been working for days.

The construction trailer was being maneuvered around and was next in line for the barge that was waiting to transport everything over to the island. Don sauntered over. He was pleased with himself; after the morning set-to with Jim everything was going according to plan.

"You look yummy in that dress, good enough to eat, I'd say."

"That is the second time today someone mentioned my dress." Isabelle retorted.

"Who was the first?" asked Don.

"Some guy at the ice cream shop."

"What was his name? Do I know him?" Don asked as he picked up a ham and cheese sandwich.

"His name was Jerry. Do you know him?"

Don froze for a second and then took a bite of the sandwich.

"No, I have never met the man." Don replied. But Isabelle thought his eyes told a different story.

*****

Jim sauntered across the ice cream shop and stopped in front of the cooler.

"What would you like, Big Jim?"

"Me, between your legs."

Ordinarily such vulgar talk would have repulsed Kate. But the twinkle in Jim's eye implied he was merely trying to get her goat. Well, she wouldn't give him her goat, or anything else either! "Never happen."

"I'll show you the world."

"Really? How are you going to do that, in your mullet boat?"

Jim laughed, and then leaned over the ice cream cooler; his red beard wiped the condensation off the stainless steel ledge.

"I'll blow the hot breath of the Sahara Desert in your ears. I'll give you wet kisses from the Aegean Sea where the sea nymphs play. I'll rub your body with olive oil from the island of Crete. I'll play music on your toes, like a Negress in Jakarta taught me. I'll massage your soul with ecstasy like they do in the Himalayas." His green eyes danced to his tune.

"When are you ever going to stop trying?"

"I'll stop when the world stops."

"If you are as good at what you say, you'd have a thousand camp followers," Kate replied.

*****

The full moon and the hot, sticky weather worked like caffeine. I can't sleep, Kate thought. The moonlight casts Salvador Dali images against the opposite wall of her sweltering bedroom.

She walked to the window. It was the witching hour of midnight; night glowed with surrealistic images and the moon played tricks on her mind. With padded feet so as not to wake her boys, Kate crept downstairs to the shop. She found a seat at the old oak table and stared out the window. A Tiffany glass lamp hung from the ceiling over the table; it was dated 1919, New York, but it wasn't signed. Kate had found the lampshade in an antique shop in Cincinnati years ago.

Light danced in and out of the fishnets on Bob's Bait House, casting shadows like fallen figures on a chessboard. The knight moves to C-4 and my queen is in jeopardy, Kate mused. She shuddered.

The moonlight was intriguing. It pulled Kate to her

feet and dragged her outside. The shell drive was warm under her feet; small bits of the crustacean surface wedged their way between her toes as she walked across the parking lot.

As she reached the pavement, she noticed the asphalt was still warm and soft with the heat of the day. Kate walked toward the Shell Creek Bridge. The silence was disturbing. There was no drone of a boat motor in the distance, no hum of an airplane, and it was too early for the far away whistle of the Arcadia train traveling south, just dead silence.

The smell of hot tar and dry wood filled her nostrils as she reached the bridge. She placed each foot carefully, avoiding the sticky tar and protruding splinters.

"Hi, lady."

Kate jumped. Down on the riprap rocks by the water's edge was Jerry, silhouetted against the jagged rocks by the moon's hard silver-white light.

"Catch anything?" she said in a stage whisper. The night's ambience compelled her to both walk and talk softly, as if daytime modes and motions would shatter the evening.

"I've had a few bites," he said softly. "It's early, though, the tide just started out."

With cautiously placed steps, she walked to the edge of the bridge and sat down, avoiding the tar. The tide was swirling around the pilings on its way out to sea. Stretching her legs, Kate was able to reach the water with her big toe. The water felt deliciously cool on her toes, teasing the rest of her body.

"Beautiful night."

"Sure is," Kate said.

"What brings you out tonight?"

"Restless, I can't sleep. It's hot."

"It's a full moon." Jerry said.

The night has a special luminosity. The palm trees formed long purple shadows that drifted over the rocks. Kate kicked at the shadows in the water with her big toe, watching them dissipate and reform.

"How did your day go?"

"Well, Big Jim came in the store and said he would blow the hot breath of the Sahara Desert in my ear."

"Is he trying to get in your knickers?"

"I guess he is,"

"Can't blame a guy for trying. Why don't you give him a turn?"

"Are you kidding? I'd have to find a clothes line big enough to hold him, scrub him down with a wire brush, then cut his hair, trim his red beard, clean his finger nails, brush his teeth, wash his clothes, dress him, powder him down, and by then I would be so exhausted and I'd be good for nothing, let alone sex."

"But just think of the fun you might have," Jerry laughed as he lit his cigarette and chucking all the while.

"But if he were debonair, cleaned up and sweet-smelling, he wouldn't be Jim."

"What? You mean you don't like big burly musky-smelling men?"

"No."

"So what's really bothering you if it's not Jim?"

"Do you remember a year ago late spring, I told you about the four men who tried to chisel down the price of crabs from the Crab Lady?"

"Yeah."

"They're developing the Key," Kate said. "And they started construction in a big way. They offered me a job assisting their homeowners with choices as to carpet, paint, tile, colors etc. Somehow they found out that I had a degree in design."

Jerry raised an eyebrow. "So you can do more than dip ice cream."

Kate smirked. "Anyway, I turned them down. Next, they offered me a quote, chance, unquote, to open an ice cream shop on the Key. They said I was local color. Me, local color, can you imagine?"

"Yes I can. And I'd say they have good taste."

"Jerry, I am serious."

"So am I. you're a smart, good-looking woman; you would give the Key some class."

"They are going to develop this area."

"People have said that for years."

"This time it will happen."

"Every fly-by-night who comes down here fishing gets to looking around and begins to think this is paradise," Jerry said. "Then they start counting the opportunities and the money they can make. I mean, this is Florida. Get-rich-quick schemes and carpetbaggers come and go like days on a calendar."

Jerry threw his fishing line into the eddy. He stood tall, a big man in his trademark navy blue. I watched him clamber over the rocks along Shell Creek. He got a strike. The fish bit hard and his pole bowed. Jerry stepped across the rocks, jumping from one to another like a two hundred pound ballerina. As he raises and lowers his fishing pole while reeling in the line, the fish does his own dance. He breaks water and shakes his head trying to rid himself of the hook.

Kate was caught up in the struggle. The high moon was at full force as it pushed the tide out the creek and caused the water to swirl around the pilings. Bits of phosphorus clung to the pilings and to Kate's feet, a diamond ring for each toe. The fish broke water again, a silvery piece of sculpture covered in glittering scales. The evening grew still.

Kate waited for the fish to rise again.

"Where did he go?"

Jerry was silent, reeling away at a frenetic pace. Suddenly there was a big splash of water where the rocks met the water's edge. The fish broke loose and followed the tide out to sea.

"Damn."

"He fought a good battle and he won." Kate teased.

"Are you kidding? There goes my dinner."

"Well, you must eat pretty late," Kate, laughed. "How can you walk across those rocks in cowboy boots without falling? I would break my neck."

"Practice." He put down his equipment and fumbled for yet another cigarette. Once he had it lit Jerry sat down and stared at Kate. "Kate, are you going to take them up on their offer and open a store on the Key?"

"No."

"Why?"

"I don't like or trust those men, if I lose the shop I will never open another ice cream store."

"What do you mean by lose?"

"Did you know that there are plans to put through an inter-coastal waterway from Tampa to Miami, and that it will go through our bay? Also, that the Corp of Engineers is—

"Wait, did you say Corp of Engineers?"

"Yes, why?'

"Now, I know we are in trouble. Those bastards have never done anything right as far as I know. If you want something fucked-up, invite the Corp of Engineers. What else was said?"

"Well, you know Roger, the mullet fisherman? He comes in for coffee early in the morning. He is working construction and his cousin works for the county and the scoop is the Corp of Engineers is going to dredge a waterway from Tampa to Miami, so that boat traffic will not have to go outside in the Gulf. The main bridges will be replaced with drawbridges and they will connect the Key to the mainland with a drawbridge. These wooden bridges, Shell Creek and Turtle Creek, will be replaced and made higher for boat traffic. The approach for the bridge will take my parking lot and part of my shop. So I am out of business."

"Who are these clowns?"

"I don't know all their names. They purchased the Crab Lady's property, too."

"Sounds to me we need a cup of coffee."

"I'll go back to the shop and make a pot."

"No, I'll treat. I bring my coffee with me." Jerry reached for his Thermos and climbed up the rocks to the bridge. Kate moved so he can sit on her right. But he motioned no and sat to her left.

"Can't hear out of my left ear, this is my good ear." He pointed to his right ear.

"Why don't you get a hearing aid?"

"Vanity."

"You're crazy, wouldn't you rather hear?"

"No."

"No one sees a hearing aid."

"No thank you, I am ugly enough."

"You are not."

Jerry fumbled with his Thermos and clumsily poured the coffee in to the lid. His hands were large, slightly swollen, and disfigured, more like the hands of a laborer with arthritis. His knuckles were huge, and every joint was puffy.

"Yes, I am ugly; my nose can't make up its mind which direction it's going. I have a permanent grin from my jaw being broken so many times, my left eye has a mind of its own, can't hear out of my left ear, and sometimes I can't find my way home."

"I think you're beautiful. Now pass me the coffee."

"It's black."

"Black is okay. So what made you move down here?"

"I wanted my anonymity. Here I am just a man who doesn't have to explain himself. I felt a freak in society where I lived; always answering questions and signing autographs.

"Don't hate me because I'm famous," Kate gave him A skeptic grin.

They both laughed.

"Yeah, you're right; there's more to it than that." Jerry paused, listening to the water lapping against the rocks.

I am a man with many addictions: to pain, women, alcohol, smoking, fame, you name it, I have an addiction to it."

"I don't believe that, Jerry, you are being too hard on yourself."

"No, I am not. When I was married there were so many women, They followed me from the ring home, waited for me after events and if, they were beautiful I had them. One Barbie Doll after another, add in the booze and the occasional drugs, I was not a likeable guy. I was never home and when I came home I was hung-over mean and miserable to live with. My wife divorced me put our daughter in a private school so she wouldn't have to see me drunk or whoring around."

Kate sat silently and listened to Jerry and sipped her black coffee.

"My worst addiction was to pain. When I was in the ring I waited for my opponent to lay one on me. It would strike some mean hidden cord with in me. I would attack him with such vengeance that I would not stop till he was face down on the floor. I almost killed a man in the ring and that was my wake-up call. I quit boxing and went for counseling. I slowly conquered my additions one at time except smoking. Then one day I open my window in my office to get some fresh air and what do I see walking down the street but a gorgeous woman. Isabelle reminds me of her; I would have to have her. I would have pursued her until I found her. What would I have done I don't know. So, I move here to try a new way of life.

Anyway, with this ugly face who would want me? I scare myself every morning when I look into the mirror and shave. Now finish telling we what is going on."

"The man I nicknamed the Alligator has bought the property south of Turtle Creek Bridge for an investment based on the Inter-coastal going through. 'Prime property,' he said."

Kate fidgeted nervously, peeling the splinters of dried wood from the edge of the old wooden bridge, as she told Jerry of her fears of losing her shop.

"You could go back home. You never told me why you came to this isolated spot."

"I am not ready to tell my story." Kate said.

"You may find the answers are in the telling."

Kate looked at Jerry again, and noticed how the boxer's craggy face was mirrored in the rough riprap at the water's edge. It was a good face, an honest one, and suddenly she had the urge to put her secrets in safe hands.

"We lived in Chicago. My husband worked at the

Merchandize Mart and we lived in the suburbs," Kate said. "It was a good life, beautiful house, good friends, and wonderful income. But the winters are mean, cold to the bone. My husband loved warm weather and every January when it is sub-zero in Chicago we would go and seek warm sunny places. Miami was and still is so commercial and phoney; we would travel to Nassau, St. Thomas, St. Croix…"

She paused, looking off into the water as if seeing her life unwind before her. "Finally we decided on Spanish Wells off the coast of Eleuthera in the Bahamas. It's a small island with a few houses, a small inn on the water with beautiful beaches, beautiful weather, quiet and not commercial. But then Hank died."

"I'm sorry to hear that," Jerry said.

"Thank you, Jerry," Kate said. "Well, after Hank died I was visiting a friend down here and he and his wife took me for a boat ride. We went to the pass and walked along northern tip of the island and I fell in love with the Gulf, the deserted beaches, the solitude of the place, and the beautiful weather. I believed I was in paradise and I still do. I moved here maybe because I believed I was fulfilling Hank's dream, or maybe I believed that moving to a place that I knew he would have loved would keep his memory alive."

"Are you still grieving for him?"

"No, I miss him, he was pretty dynamic sort of person, but what's gone is gone. Besides, I have my hands full with the boys and the shop; I don't have time to grieve."

"Well, you shouldn't make a career out of it, but it's

good to grieve now and then.

"What makes you so smart?"

"Too many blows to the head." Jerry laughed and stared down at his hands. He flexed his fists several times; after a few moments he asked.

"Will you stay?"

"I don't know. If they start to dredge a channel tomorrow, how long do you think it would take to finish?"

"A year, maybe two, depending where they start."

"Jer, maybe, we have time," Kate said. What will the Crab Lady do? What will we all do if they really put through the waterway?"

It's hard to give up something you have worked a lifetime for, especially land, Kate thought. Land has a quality of ownership like nothing else. She recalled the time, when she was a girl, she saw her father leaning against his hoe. The afternoon sun silhouetted him, and he loomed tall. He reached down and scooped a handful of dirt, he smelled the soil and then he did a most peculiar thing: he tasted the dirt. He nodded a yes, then fingered the dirt that was left in his hand and let the wind take the rest. He died three days later.

"Kate, you forget that time has stood still here for so long, we don't realize there is a world outside of Shell Creek," Jerry said. "We're untouched by reality. We live in a world of self-gratification that compares to nowhere else in the world. We live as we choose. We drink as we please, and fight when it makes us happy. There is no law; the closest law is thirty-five miles north and forty miles south. We govern ourselves, and we do a damned good job. We are unregulated by anything. Most of us live in shacks without running water, not by design but by choice."

Jerry put his hand on Kate's shoulder. They sat and watched the tide rush out and the water swirl around the pilings. The full moon was high, and the rocks glowed with inner light. Specks of phosphorous clung to the rocks refusing to die. Thousands of diamonds washed on the riprap and slid slowly off the rocks and lost themselves in the shadows of the palm trees.

Bob's Old Bait Shack - 1979

Shrimp and Sweet Potato Pie

On a rare day in Southwest Florida, with cloudy skies, a slight drizzle of rain, temperature about seventy-two degrees, and a little humidly--- Kate had just finished her daily chores and was standing in front of the window watching the raindrops fall. Across the road business neighbor, Bob of Bob's Bait house; was outside taking down the fish net and removing the colorful floats. She watched him take the colorful paddles out of his mullet boat. Why was he doing that? Kate wondered as he gathered up the fishing net, folded it, and put the floats into a bag. Then he stepped across the road and came into the Ice Cream Shop.

"Hi, Kate?"

"Yes."

"I'm Bob, I know we've never met, I've been across the street from you for the last couple years," he said. He offered her the bag of floats and nets. "I thought you might want these things."

"I don't know what to say. Why are you giving these away?"

"I've sold the bait house and the property. I know this is a hell of a way to meet."

"Would you like a cup of coffee, my treat?"

"Why not?" he said, "I need a break from packing."

"Thought your business was doing well, according to all the fishermen who come in here for coffee."

"I sold the property; I had an offer I could not refuse."

Kate made two cups of coffee and carried them over to a small table. "Cream and sugar?"

"Just cream. Thanks."

"Did you sell your property to Don Buyers?"

"No, actually I sold the property to the county."

"The county? Why would they want your piece of land?"

"Well, with all the developing going on south of here, there's no place for the public to launch a boat. The county is going to replace the bridges—you know that." Kate nodded. "They offered to buy my place for a public boat launch. The offer was so generous I could not refuse. They made a sketch of sorts showing the boat launch, a public facility, parking lot and I believe a couple of picnic tables. If I had refused they would take the land by eminent domain. I don't believe that Don

Buyers knows that I have sold or he would have been knocking on my door. The County will be sending surveyors soon to start the project."

"Eminent domain? No one has approached me about buying land," Kate said. "I know that I am going to lose part of my driveway and parking lot, but the county hasn't offered any money."

"Because, the former owners sold that to the county before you purchased this parcel" Bob said. He scratched his baldhead, and then leaned forward. "You bought this from Cagey Ernie, a slick old cracker. His family has been here since the last century and they owned all the land around here. The county's been talking about replacing the bridges for years, so when they got serious he started selling. No one wanted my piece of property because it is full of mangroves and pepper trees and water is shallow, good for mullet boats and mullet fishermen. But, there are some good fishing holes where the mangrove snappers hide and the grass flats are good trout fishing, even though the water is hard to navigate. So I bought at a good price. Hey, how much for a refill?" he asked, wagging his cup.

"On the house," Kate said, eager to pump her once-silent neighbor for more info.

"Now your side of road that backs up to bay with deep-water access is more valuable," he said. "Cagey Ernie, that's what we called him back then; his wife was a real estate broker. So he sold the piece of land that was under eminent domain to the county and you bought the rest. He did the same thing with property next to yours;

sold the eminent domain to the county and the rest to that boxer. Then the boxer purchased the shacks and Ernie didn't tell him there's is an eagle's nest on the property."

"What boxer? Are you talking about Jerry?"

"I don't know his name."

"So, where is Cagey Ernie?" Kate asked.

"He and his wife moved to Alabama after he sold the turpentine shacks."

"I wonder why Alabama?"

"He said there would be too many people here."

"Are you going to stay or move?"

"Me? Hell, I'm going to Alabama too, for the same reason. When Don Buyers get through here there will be too many people. I'm closter phobic." Bob continued, he took another sip of coffee, and then smacked his lips.

"It is a shame Kate, that after two years I finally get aquatinted with my neighbor. Tell me how did you find this place and why are you here?"

Kate explained that she and her husband had been looking for an escape from the Windy City.

"My kids have blossomed here," she said. "They learned to fish and boat. Steven and Philip have explored every island, creek and river, they know every fishing hole. They both are excellent swimmers. They can read navigation charts, Philip has learned to dive and will be certified next month, and they're planning to go the Keys for sportsmen's weekend to dive for lobster." Kate laughed. "We've fished for every fish in the Gulf, they netted, gigged, trolled, trapped, hooked, and dug everything from trout, flounder, clams, oysters, to shook. They would never have had those experiences in Chicago. Only thing we have not fished for has been shrimp."

"What? You've never been shrimping?"

"No, I've always wanted to go, but we don't have a shrimp net, and I don't know what is involved.

Bob sat back in his chair and drummed his fingers on the table. "Tomorrow is a full moon and there's gonna be an outgoing tide. Tell you what: I'll show you and your boys how to catch shrimp. You're gonna want to get a nine-volt battery, two anchor lines—one for the bow and the other for the stern. I'll bring the shrimp nets, spotlights, and the five-gallon buckets." He grew more animated as he planned the adventure. "You bring the drinks; we'll go out at sunset. Don't forget to tell your son he needs two anchors."

Bob stood up and took the last swallow of his coffee. "Well, gotta get back to packing," he said. "See you tomorrow."

*****

Steven and Philip just walked in the door from school and were helping Kate clean up when Bob rushed into the Ice Cream Shop.

"Are you ready for tonight?"

Funny, Kate thought, I've been here for almost two years and have never spoken to him before and now when he's moving. I see him several times in one day.

"Yes, I think so. I'm packing a thermos of coffee,

sandwiches, and peanut butter cookies that I made today."

"I recognize your boys," Bob said, "Steven you're the big guy with the boat, right?"

"Yes sir," Steven said. "Mom gave us a list of what we need—I think I got everything."

"I want to go too" Philip chimed in.

"You're in, chief," Bob gave him a big smile.

"Great, we'll have a blast," Philip said.

"What we need is a nine volt battery, two spot lights, several five-gallon buckets, an anchor, and some shrimp nets," Bob said, ticking off the list of essentials again. "My nets are all packed"

"We have an extra anchor, one spot light, and I have four five-gallon buckets," Steven said.

"And don't forget, we can use the nets you gave me yesterday," Kate said.

"Steve, let's go and ask Jerry, bet he has some of these things," Philip said. "He owes you one, remember? Let's go and collect.

"Give me a few minutes while I finish making sandwiches. I'll drive you down," Kate said.

"Okay Mom, I'll meet you at the car—hey Philip, you coming?"

"Are you kidding? Of course I'm coming."

Kate wrapped the sandwiches in wax paper and put them in the refrigerator and went outside to drive the kids to Jerry's.

"I'll get my gear together and wait for you guys," Bob said as Kate drove off.

At Jerry's Steven told Kate and Philip to wait as he went up to the house.

"What's with him?" Philip asked.

Right then, Kate realized that Jerry had became a father image for Steven. Small wonder, she thought, it wasn't as if he'd had a male in his life, not since Hank died. She knew Steven was approaching the age when he needed someone, a man and mentor to model his behavior on, or just to tell him about the birds and bees. She did not relish the thought about having that talk with him.

"Mom?" Phillip interrupted her thought. "I said, what's up with Steven?"

"He and Jerry are good friends, Phillip," Kate said.

Philip was about to speak, but Steven and Jerry came up to the car and interrupted him.

"Hi Lady. Heard you're going shrimping."

"That's right," Kate said. "Bob is taking us shrimping tonight and we'd like to borrow some equipment."

"Bob? Bob's Bait Shop Bob?"

"That's the one," Kate said.

"He sort of keeps to himself," Jerry said. "He finally succumbs to your beauty?"

Steven and Philip laughed as Kate blushed.

"All jokes aside, Lady, what do you need?"

"I thought you might have a nine volt battery and a spot light we could borrow," Kate said.

"Come on you guys, let's take a look,"

A few minutes later Jerry and Steve came back. Not carrying just one battery but three. Also four spotlights and paraphernalia for attaching the lights to the gunnels of the boat. They put the stuff in the trunk of the car.

"I owe you one, Jerry" Steve said.

"Forget it Steve you don't owe me anything."

"Oh, yes, I do."

"No, you don't just go and have fun."

"Thank you very much Jerry," Kate said. "We'll take good care of your things and bring them back tomorrow."

Jerry nodded and waved good-bye and yelled, "Catch you later."

"I thought we would be there all night with your 'owe you, no, you owe me nothing' routine," said Philip.

"Stuff it, squirt," Steven said. "Jerry would give you literally the shirt off his back and not expect anything back. Anyway, it is a kind of game we play."

"Some game," Philip remarked.

Kate dropped the boys off at Bob's.

"Help Bob load the boat and I will get the food."

After much debate they decided to take Bob's boat. It was wider and larger then Steven's; not only that the gunnels were higher and Bob thought it would be safer. They started for the pass about six thirty. Sunset would not be for another hour or so, but Bob wanted an early start and time to position his boat in the pass before the tide turned.

They scooted quickly through Ski Alley and slowed down to an idle speed as they entered the pass.

"My God, it's a parking lot!" Kate exclaimed. It seemed as if everyone in town who had a boat was at the pass. They were all lined up with the boats facing the Gulf and spotlights clamped to the gunnels. Kate heard music playing from one boat. Folks were laughing, drinking, eating, and just plain old having fun.

"In case you didn't notice, the whole area of Shell Creek is here," Bob said, stating the obvious. "It's a rare occurrence to have a full moon with an outgoing tide. The shrimp will be plentiful and they'll be moving fast. Once they start their run for the Gulf we won't have time for anything else but dip for shrimp.

"That is the reason I wanted to leave early," Bob said."

As he started to maneuver the boat he barked orders to Steve and Philip

"Get the anchors out. Throw out the bow anchor. Make sure the line is tight; make sure it is secure. Now throw the stern anchor. Same thing, make sure you have a good hold, make it tight and secure. When the tide changes, it will come through the pass fast and furious. We don't want the boat drifting to either side."

Once the boat was lined up in the pass they started to set up the lights. Kate just sat on the gunnel in the stern of the boat and watched. It was fascinating. First they put two nine-volt batteries on the port side and two on the starboard side. They hooked the wires to the terminals, like hooking up a car battery charger, and then plugged the cords into the spotlights. Then they clamped the spotlights to the gunnels of the boat. Bob adjusted each light and tightened the clamps. The boys caught on fast as they watched Bob with adept attention. Kate could hear and see the wheels turning in their minds. Bob turned the lights on and off a couple of times 'til he was confident that everything was working.

Bob turned off the engine, and then he checked the lines. "Good work boys, I can see you have experience."

"Kate, would you pour me a cup of coffee."

"Sure."

Bob checked his watch and checked the water that flowed by the bow of boat. Then he leaned against the steering wheel and sipped his coffee.

"We have half an hour before tide change," he said. "Philip and Steve you'll work the tide from the port side your Mom will work the tide from the starboard side. I'm not going to dip. I am going to help and watch you have fun."

The boys moved to port, ready for action.

"Steve I want you to watch the stern anchor. I don't want it to come loose. Philip likewise you watch the bowline. You each have a shrimp net; the best way is to just let the shrimp swim into the net. There's a funnel at the end and once they are in the net they can't swim out. You don't need to reach out over the boat they will swim right by. The current will be swift and I don't want anyone over board. Any questions?"

Kate and the boys shook their heads, even as. she fought an urge to salute.

"If not," Bob said, "let's eat."

Kate took out the sandwiches, the cookies, and chip, some soft drinks. A general stir among the other boats cut the meal short—the shrimp were running!

Philip turned on his spotlight and he saw the first shrimp float up to the surface. He grabbed his shrimp net and as he tried to put the pole in the water he gave Bob a tap on the head. Bob laughed, but it took a while for Kate and the boys to get used to the pole and the dipping routine.

They dipped the shrimp for hours until all four of the five-gallon buckets were full. They were exhausted but the boys still did not want to quit.

"It's close to midnight," boys, Kate said. "You know you have school tomorrow."

The shrimp were still running.

"What am I going to do with all these shrimp?" Kate asked.

"Give them away or freeze them," Bob said.

"Eat them." Philip and Steven said in unison.

"Let's go home and cook some now," Steven said.

"You have school tomorrow."

"So, how long does it take cook shrimp?" asked Philip.

"Two minutes," Bob spoke up.

"Is that right? I've never cooked shrimp," Kate said. "When we lived in Chicago I bought them frozen."

"Well if you want to cook them, I'll show you how," Bob said.

"That settles that, we are going to eat shrimp tonight." Steven said.

Later, while Bob, Steven, and Philip cleaned the boat and washed the salt water off everything, Kate put a large pot of water on to boil shrimp. She looked down at the grey squirming shrimp and decided to let the kids do the dirty work. It took them longer to clean the boat than it did for the water to boil, so she put it on simmer and started setting a table in the ice cream shop. The door opened and Kate heard a familiar voice.

"Hi Lady, you're open late," Jerry said.

"You just stopped by because you knew I would be cooking shrimp."

"I saw the lights on and I thought I'd check to see if everything went well."

"It did. I never had so much fun in my life catching those shrimp," Kate said. "You might as well stay. We're going to cook those critters. We have four five-gallon buckets full of shrimp and you could take some home."

"Well, I would say you did well."

"Would you like a cup of coffee if I make a pot?"

"Yes."

At that moment the boys and Bob came in, carrying the rest of the shrimp and a six-pack of beer.

"I'm ready for my lesson on how to cook these little creatures," Kate said.

She introduced Jerry to Bob. Then Kate put on a pot of coffee and Bob showed her how to cook shrimp. He insisted that the shrimp were better if you cooked them with their head on because they taste better.

"You can serve them with heads on or cut them off, either way," he said.

Kate and the boys decided to leave the heads on.

Bob opened two cans of beer and poured them into the water before he put the shrimp in the pot and he cooked them exactly to two minutes, after which he drained off the water and put the pot on the table. Kate plunked down some cocktail sauce and a large roll of paper towels.

"Delicious," Kate exclaimed. Her decision was unanimous.

After the boys went to bed, Jerry, Bob, and Kate sat around and chatted.

"Are you the boxer that owns the point?" Bob asked Jerry.

"Yep, why do you ask?"

"When I sold my property to the county they said a boxer bought the point and that you're planning to develop the land."

"No, I bought the land for an investment, but now I can't do anything while the eagles are nesting. That could be years down the road."

"That piece of land is beautiful and the point with its hundred-and-eighty-degree view is something else."

"I know," Jerry whispered.

"You could always sell it to Don Buyers," Bob teased with a devilish look on his face.

"That is one thing I'm not going to do," Jerry vowed. "I will give the land away before Don Buyers gets his hands on that point."

"He has his minions already looking around," Bob said.

"Who would that be?" ask Kate.

"A man named Harold Greenburg from Chicago," Bob said. "Greenburg is Buyers' attorney."

"Like I said before, I will never sell to Don regardless. I will give land to the state for a park, first!" Jerry stated.

The men sat and sipped some more of the beer as Kate busied herself cleaning up. Bob, who said earlier he was packed and ready to leave town, seemed to want to stick around.

"By the way, Jerry, how did you become the heavyweight champion?" Bob asked out of the blue.

"Sweet potato pie."

"Sweet potato pie?' Kate asked.

"You got to be kidding." Bob said. "Tell me about it."

Both Kate and Bob leaned back in their chairs.

"I grew up in Cleveland," Jerry said. "Cleveland is very ethnic city, the whole east side is divided into ethnic areas; there is the Jewish neighborhood, the Italians, the Colored, the Polish, the Hungarian, and the Irish sections. The Colored, Italian and the Jewish neighborhoods butted together. The street we lived on was integrated; three colored families lived across the street from our house. We never socialized with them, not even a hello or good morning; they kept to themselves and so did we.

"My dad worked in the steel mills, stoking a blast furnace. He came down with pneumonia, which developed into black lung. So they put him the hospital, which put my mom and my six brothers and sisters in a pinch. One day a black woman, one of our neighbors, showed up on our doorstep with a sweet potato pie she had baked. She knew my dad was in the hospital; she was concerned and wanted help."

"Hey, hold on," Bob interrupted. "What does a sweet potato pie have to do with boxing?"

"If you have any patience I'll get to that in a minute," Jerry said. He was in full story-telling mode and was not to be rushed.

"So a few days later, my mom made some Italian cookies and sent me next door to return the favor. I ran into two colored guys playing hoops outside and they asked me to join them. Their father wanted his sons to play sports so they could land a scholarship for college. Well, one thing led to another and we started playing sports together. They had a chance to compete in a boxing tournament and one of the high school coaches said he'd coach 'em for free. They didn't like boxing but I took to it like a duck to water. Next thing you know, I won a Golden Gloves championship and I was on my way, thanks to a sweet potato pie. If Mrs. O'Dell had not brought the sweet potato pie my life story would be a lot different."

Before Kate or Bob could ask any questions, Jerry went on with his story. "James went to college on a basketball scholarship and I boxed myself up the ranks. James O'Dell and I became close friends. We own a Gym in Brooklyn and we try to help under pledged kids."

*****

That night Kate dreamt about shrimp. She dreamed she was swimming with the shrimp and was floating down the funnel with the shrimp and sweet potato pie. Then she woke up.

"Oh my God," she said out loud. "I have all those shrimp to put in the freezer. First I need a cup of coffee, which would be what the doctor ordered."

As she was putting the coffee pot on there was a knocking at her door. Roger, Dwayne and Chappie came in for their morning coffee. They were down in the mouth this morning.

"Today is Bob's last day, he's already packed his truck an' it is full to the gills." Roger said.

"Where are we gonna buy bait now?' Dwayne moaned. "Bob said there was a shop by the old bridge that goes to the beach," Roger answered.

"It won't be the same. Nothin' will ever be the same once they start cuttin' up the land." Chappie moaned.

"You're probably right Dwayne, but I am going to make the best of it." Roger said.

"Yeah, you turn tail, you will just keep on working for Don Buyers." Accused Chappie.

"Well, it's a job." Roger was a little defensive about working for Buyers, particularly after Chappie and Dwayne had begun calling him a sell-out. "These days, it looks like every dog's gotta start learning some new tricks. Not only do we have all this buildin' happenin' but the state's been threatenin' to put a ban on netting for mullet because they are becoming extinct"

"Man, at one time we had so much mullet they would jump in to your boat, no kiddin'" Chappie said. "

"I hear them jump if I have the windows open," Kate said. "It's kind of musical."

"Yeah? Well if they put that ban in, it'll be the end of that tune," Harold said with a glum expression. "It'll kill us, most of us make a living during mullet season. It can be very lucrative."

"When does mullet season begin?" asked Kate.

"Usually about now, you start to cast net in August but if you wait for cold weather the fish are fatter and they bring more money at market," Roger said. "Price goes from fifty cents a pound to eighty cents a pound; day-to-day; the fatter the fish the more money. The biggest market is the Japanese, they love mullet, they only eat the roe; the rest they throw away."

"That's a damn shame too, a waste of good fish," Chappie said.

"I've seen those Japanese trawlers in the Gulf netting for mullet," Harold added. "That's who the state should be going after, not fellas like us just tryin' to make a livin'.

"The Japanese are in International waters, they're allowed. Dwayne cried.

"After you catch these fish where do you take them?" Kate asked.

"We take them to the Fishery down in Placida, the owner buys them from us then sells them on the open market."

Kate listened to the fishermen bitch and moan for a while, and then she remembered how the whole conversation got started. "Oh. I almost forgot," she said. "I have a package of sandwiches and stuff for Bob's trip; you fellas mind helping yourselves while I run it over to Bob?"

Kate had packed a few sandwiches, several bags of fresh-cooked shrimp, cookies, and soft drinks into a throwaway cooler. As Kate walked across the street, she also noticed that Roger was right; Bob's pick-up truck was full of equipment ready for the trip to Alabama.

"You're up early this morning," Bob said. "I'm surprised, we had a late night."

"I could not sleep, I was thinking about freezing the rest of the shrimp."

"Did you freeze them with their head still in place?"

"Yep, that's what you said, right?" Asked Kate. "Anyway, I brought you a care package for the road, a big boy's lunch."

"Thank you.'

"How long is the drive to Alabama?

"Twelve to fifteen hours... depends on how many stops I make."

"Please be careful and visit sometimes."

"I will."

"Well, I left the boys talking stuff and drinking up my coffee," Kate said, "I better get back over there."

"See ya, neighbor," Bob said as he waved goodbye.

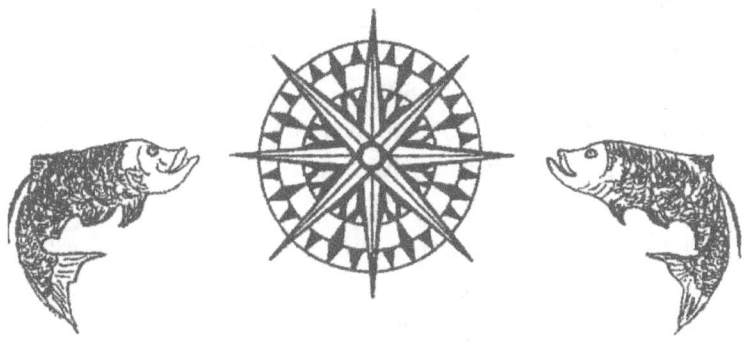

A Raccoon and A Bulldozer

S everal months later, on the first day of spring break Steven and Philip raced out of the Ice Cream Shop at the break of dawn. Steven had heard about a new fishing spot and he wanted to try it out. As he passed the table where the fishermen usually camped, Chappie called out to him," Hey young man, going to catch some big ones today?"

"Uh. No, we're just goin' down to look for arrowheads at the Indian Mound," Steven said.

"You boys be careful," Kate said.

"Okay, Mom," Philip answered. When they got down

to the dock, Philip turned to his brother. "Steven, why'd you tell Chappie that, I thought we were goin' to this new fishing hole you found."

"We are," Steven said. He looked a little embarrassed about lying. "But the last time I told them about a spot I found they fished it out."

Philip laughed. Soon the boys were on the water. It was so early, Steven felt sort of bad about gunning the engine. Instead he just followed the current, or let the engine on troll intermittently. Soon they had cleared the point.

"Look for a pepper tree that looks like it just got a crew-cut," Steven yelled.

"There it is," Philip called out moments later.

"Okay," Steven said. He began counting the inlets, at the third one he turned the tiller and the boat began heading into a murky area lined with mangroves. After a short distance, the brackish water gave way to a pool so clear; one could see the bottom, and schools of redfish.

"All mine—" Steven exulted, but then he remembered Philip "—ours."

"Good morning, young fellas," someone shouted out.

Off to the boys' left was a small skiff containing a guy the locals called "The Professor." He wore one of those cancer hats, a chapeau that started at the back of his neck, covered the ears, and came almost down to his nose. As usual, he wore a stained, wrinkled seersucker suit, dirty white shirt, and a tie. "Welcome to my world," he called out gleefully.

"So much for your secret spot," Philip smirked.

Soon The Professor had edged his boat to Steven's, then launched into a monologue about fishing.

"We might as well be back in school," groused Steven as the old eccentric chattered on.

"Fishing resembles life at its core."

"Teach a man to fish and he will never go hungry." Philip interjected.

"Do you fish?" the Professor asked, as if oblivious to the boys' gear. "It is life at is core."

Steven shook his head. "No."

"When you fish you throw your baited line in the water, sooner or later a fish will swim by, see the bait, make a few passes, it might nudge the fish and if you're SENSITIVE you will feel the nudge. A good fisherman then pulls his bait away. The fish will swim away, but it will come back again and this time you let him smell the bait and you give it a little wiggle.

The boys looked at one another, and then began slowly easing their boat away from the man.

"He, the fish, will then nibble to see if the bait is worthy of him," the Professor said, holding onto the gunnels of the boys' boat as if buttonholing them. "When he smells the bait, it will drive him crazy. It's the pheromone that drives him crazy. The tribes in Africa knew of the power of the aphrodisiacs and still do. Since the beginning of time hunters have killed the rhinoceros for his horn, one of the most powerful aphrodisiacs. When the fish smells that, he will bite with such ferociousness, that all you need to do his reel him, if you can."

As if on cue, The Professor's line grew taut and his rod began to bow. As he struggled with an apparent catch, Steven slowly trolled away.

"Pheromones?" he asked, shaking his head. "What do you think of that?"

Philip looked sort of thoughtful as he gazed out over the water. "I think I'm going to get me a girlfriend," he said.

"Let's plan a trip to Africa." said Steven, with a grin.

Hours later, after dinner, Philip drew Steven aside. "Hey, you want to go hang out?" he asked.

"Where?" Steven asked. "There's nothing much to do around here."

"Jim was telling me about the Liar's Club," Philip said.

"What's that?"

Once a month, all the old guys in town get together over a campfire down on Don Pedro Island and tell stories," Philip said.

"A campfire? In March? Oh, come on," Steven said. "I might as well go find The Professor and let him entertain me."

"Hey, what the heck" Philip said. "They don't have to have a fire. But do you want to wait around here ''til Mom asks us to help clean out the coolers or something?"

Steven thought for a moment. "Okay," he said, but this had better be good."

As the sun set, Steven and Philip pulled up at Don Pedro a little way down the bay from their home.

As they landed they ran into the fishermen who spent

many a morning in the Ice Cream Shop.

"Whaddya know?" Dwayne said. "It's the ice cream boys!"

"Dwayne, do you ever replace that cigar?" "Hi boys." said Roger.

Roger looked up from where he was sitting and motioned the boys over. "Hey fellas, sit down. Harold's jus' gettin' started."

Harold took a long swig out of a bottle wrapped in a brown paper bag, then passed it to his left. Steven made as if to take it, but Chappie adroitly plucked it out of his hands. "That ain't root beer in that bottle, son," he said. Your mom will have all of us hangin from a yardarm if she found out we been corruptin' you two."

"I was out at one a' those fishing shacks with Chappie, Big Jim and Roger back during mullet season," Harold began, "As we are drinking our morning coffee we noticed a nest of baby raccoons. Mom was not there. So Chappie came up with a bright idea—let's hide the nest and see if momma appears."

"Uh oh," said one of them men gathered in a circle.

"That's right," Harold said. "She dropped a dead lizard she had in her mouth and let out a scream that would have paralyzed a deaf man. She jumped on Chappie and started bitin' and clawin' at his back. We finally got Chappie's jacket off; he threw it and the raccoons across the room. All four of us ran for our lives out the door and jumped into Big Jim's boat and lit out like the devil himself was after us. We dropped the anchor at a safe distance and decided to watch.

"The raccoon tore that shack apart. I mean, momma broke dishes emptied cups, ripped the sheets off the cots and tore open the pillows, ripped the blankets into sheds. All the while she was screamin'. Finally she heard her cubs answer an' she was out the door tearin' apart the fishing nets where they were hidden. After the happy reunion she carried each one back into shack. The mystery is how did she get to the fishin' shack in the first place?"

"She swam." Said Roger.

"She probably did a back stroke, that way she didn't get her face wet." Steven made a smart-ass remark. "What's funnier is that all you big macho guys were afraid of that little raccoon," Steve continued

"That raccoon wasn't on your back bitin and scatchin," complained Chappie.

"I may be the youngest in the glue factory, but even I know you don't play games with a raccoon." Interrupted Philip.

"Aye, that's the famous raccoon that did a back stroke across the bay?" Steven enjoyed himself picking on the men who fished out the redfish hole.

More bottles appeared and the stories flowed. Dwayne shared his love story.

"How long have you been down here Steve?"

"About two years," Steven said.

"You got a girl friend?

Both boys shook their heads, no.

"You should. When I was your age I had a girlfriend that lived on the mainland, I live here on this island and I

Gasparilla Island Beacon - circa 1986

would swim over after my parents went to bed and she would meet me there on that beach under the beacon light." He pointed to a sandy cove across the waterway. "She would sneak out of her house and bring a blanket. We would lie on the blanket and I'd smell the lavender that she washed her hair with. I memorized a few lines from Walt Whitman and whisper the words in her ear."

"Hold on there Dwayne, you mean Walt Disney, dontcha??"

"Nope, I don't! I woulda memorized alla the volume's of Shakespeare if I had to, she was some girl.

"Anyway, the smell of her would arouse me and we'd make love all night. Just before dawn we'd go for swim and we'd both sneak home. Remember, you can fish for food but you can also fish for love."

Roger shook is head, "Love can make a man crazy, but it is sooo good. Tell me Dwayne how did you do all that kissin' and smoochin' with that cigar in your mouth?"

"Simple, at seventeen I didn't need a pacifier."

They all laughed and joked and teased Dwayne. But they became nostalgic about their first love.

As the night vultures started chirping, Philip's head began to bob. He looked over at Steven.

"Hey, ready to call it a night?" he asked.

Soon they were back in the boat, running against the current as they rounded the point.

"Well, what the hell?" Steven said. "That was a lot better than The Professor's stories."

"Still think I'm gonna find a girlfriend," Philip fantasized.

The Price of Crabs

*****

Kate was up early and hard at work on her chores in the ice cream parlor when, for second time this year she heard the sound of a bulldozer. The first time they came to raze the turpentine shacks. Now the state sent in the bulldozer to raze Bob's Bait houses. We'll have a boat launch across the street, she thought, and that may not be a bad thing.

After people finished boating it would be a natural for them to want an ice cream after a long hot day on the water. But she knew that she would be next; it was just a matter of time before the bulldozer would come for the Ice Cream Shop.

"Hi Lady, you have a lot of action across the street," Jerry said as he moseyed in.

"Yep, there goes Bob's Bait House. Coffee?"

"Please. When did this they start?"

"About an hour ago."

"Hmm looks interesting." Jerry motioned toward the window.

Harold, Dwayne, Roger and Chappie, were already drinking their coffee. The four fishermen were early this morning.

"Hey Jerry, why don't you join us?" Roger said.

"I don't mind if I do," he said. "What, no fishing today?"

"We were headed out when we stopped for coffee

and we decided to stay and watch the action across the street."

"Who's doing the demolishing?" Jerry asked.

"We don't know."

"Don Buyers was responsible for bulldozing the turpentine shacks to make room for his condominiums. I don't know who is responsible here," Dwayne said.

"Kate, can you give me another cup of coffee to go?" asked Jerry.

"Sure, you want anything with it?"

"Hand me a couple of packs of sugar and two small creamers, please."

"Sure," Kate said and gave Jerry the coffee, sugar, and creamer. "You want yours topped off? Anyone else need their coffee topped?"

All four fishermen took fill-ups, and then followed Jerry out the door.

From inside Kate watch them walk across the road and flag the guy who was running the bulldozer. He turned off the machine and jumped down as Jerry handed him a coffee. Jerry offered him a cigarette. All five stood talking, pointing in this direction and then in the other direction. The guy pointed to the old bridge and at my shop and back again to the bridge.

They ventured around the back of what was left of Bob's Bait House and disappeared. They finally came back around the other side, arms waving and fingers pointing. Roger, Harold, Dwayne and Chappie walked down the hill until all Kate could see was the top of their heads. She decided to go see for herself what was going on. But just as she placed her "GONE FISHING" sign on the door, when the men all marched single file into the shop.

"Well?" She said.

"Have you been there?" Jerry asked.

"No, why?"

"Like dyin' and goin' to heaven if you're a fisherman," said Dwayne, slightly out of breadth.

"There's this lagoon behind the Bait House that none of us have seen before," Harold said. "It's got several channels going in four directions. I wonder if Bob knew he had such a treasure? Once they cleared the brush and a couple of falling down shacks, there it was. The dozer operator said they're gonna replace the bridge over Shell Creek."

"I already knew that, Kate said.

"But did you know about the state is also replacin' the bridge on the other side of the lagoon?" Chappie spoke up. "That guy said it will make all the waterways accessible by boat for miles east of that bridge and all the land will be available for buildin' an' developin'. He also said the surveyors are beginning nex' month to stake out the new road an' the bridges."

"Kate, he said you won't lose your shop, just ten feet of road frontage, your front yard, drive way and parking lot, but you'll probably be out of business for at least two years," Dwayne said, shaking his head.

Kate was stunned. "No one has said any of this to me."

"I think it is about time for you to start asking questions," Jerry said.

151

Revelations

*I*sabelle pulled a fashionable sundress from her closet, scrutinized the dress, and then remembered Jerry's "kept woman" comment. She put the dress back in the closet and decided on a more conservative garment. But it wasn't her style so she threw it one on the bed.

She went in the closet again and grabbed the first dress she had. "Mmm, this dress should make a bull dog bite his chain." She held the garment across herself and danced around her bedroom; then stopped abruptly. Remembering Jerry's statement, she threw the dress down and lit a cigarette.

"This is bullshit," she said. "What am I doing, trying to seduce Don or please Jerry?" She started to think. When was the last time I had an actual date with Don? The last time was the Pump Room that was more then a year ago. All we do is have martinis and sex. That is not dating, it is being on call. Will he ever ask me to marry him?

In the pit of her stomach she felt a slow turning in her gut. Why am I here? Because, I know nothing else. But he pays the rent and he buys me nice things. He gave me a job. Or did he give me a job? I am an errand boy, a gal Friday, whatever, make me a martini, get me this, get me that, go fetch Jim, go find Roger, call Harold and the list goes on and on. Isabelle sat on the edge of her bed for a minute and then decides she needed to talk to someone.

Kate was replacing her supplies behind the coolers when the bells on her front door jingled. In walked Isabelle.

"Good morning, you're up early. Would you like a cup of coffee?"

"Yes, I would. Kate what do you know about sophistication?"

"Wow. That is a heavy subject this early in the morning. All I know is that some people have it and others don't. Why do you ask?"

"Well Kate, I have been thinking about what makes a person sophisticated."

"I really don't know, but my Italian grandfather

would say that some people are born sophisticated, some are raised that way from the time they are born, like the royal family in England. For instance, look at the Crab Lady. She is more sophisticated in her overalls and yellow fishing booths than someone dressed to the nines having dinner at the Waldorf Astoria.

"That ugly man said I was a kept women."

"What ugly man?"

"You know, what's his name?" Isabelle insisted.

"You don't mean Jerry? I don't think he is ugly."

Isabelle was in deep thought, something was bothering her and Kate could see the struggle. I'd better be careful what I say, she thought.

How long have you been dating Don?"

"I just graduated from high school. I was seventeen."

"What did you like about him?"

"He was handsome, tall, muscular. He drove a sport car, and he had money. I know I was just an amusement for him. He took me to the amusement park and I   enjoyed the ride."

"Do you like the same things in him? Has he asked you to marry him? What about his personality?"

Isabelle stood there biting her lower lip and but saying absolutely nothing.

"Would you like a refill on your coffee?"

"No, I think I'll go. I have a few things I have to do."

"Wait Isabelle, Why don't you try to be independent from Don?"

"How?"

"Get a job. Have you ever thought of Real Estate?

You'll need to get a license, but that shouldn't be too hard. Just think, then he'll be dependent on you to sell his houses, condos, and land."

Isabelle left the Ice Cream Shop and went back to her rented villa. There she sat on the lanai and smoked a cigarette and she felt a depression start to creep over her. She walked to her closet and started going through her clothes. She took one cocktail dress after another and threw them on the bed. She did the same with her designer high heels.

Isabelle took the mink wrap that Don bought her. A mink in Florida? She wrapped herself in it, walked to the mirror, and examined herself.

"I'll never wear this down here," she said to herself and threw it on the heap. She went through the rest of her closet again, keeping only casual clothes, things that did not make her look like a kept women.

*****

Kate walked across the road to satisfy her curiosity. The bulldozer had pushed all the debris into piles of brush, old crab traps, and other wreckage from the Bait Shop. Nothing was left standing except an injured palmetto. She felt depressed. It reminded her of the wreckage of the old turpentine shacks when Don Buyers or was that Jerry who cleared that land a year ago. Now nothing remained of the quaint old bait shop with its colorful fishnets and floats hanging on the walls. Even the old mullet boat with its painted crab traps and oars was gone, smashed to bits.

He didn't leave a fucking tree standing. Just a half dead palmetto, she thought, which he probably forgot and was too lazy to go back and finish off. Just like the bougainvillea they left behind when they destroyed the turpentine shacks.

She walked to the water's edge. The sun was beginning to set and cast a beautiful magenta glow across the water. Bait fish scurried here and there while a large snook chased them for his supper. Kate noticed the water was not very deep. She could see bottom clearly. She watched the water swirl around the pilings where Jerry always fished. Funny, she thought, how could they get a boat under that bridge at high tide—or low tide for the matter? The water was too shallow for low tide and the bridge was too low for high tide.

My God, how high is that bridge going to be? They'll have to dredge to make the water navigable at low tide and raise that bridge high enough at high tide. That would be no small project. What had Don Buyers started?

Kate began to add it all up: He had to know about the waterway and bayous and he had to make some kind of deal with the state or county or both. Let me think a second, she pondered, we're talking about four, maybe five bridges high enough for a boat with a Bimini top to pass under during high tide, a new road, paved the shell roads, and God knows what else; we are talking millions of dollars.

She turned again and looked at the Shell Creek Bridge and then followed her line of sight to the bridge that crossed under the state road and then beyond the bridge. Then it hit her, like a brick to the chest. The expanse of virgin land went beyond the old bridge both north and south and especially east. There must be hundreds of small streams, isthmuses, and lagoons that could be easily connected with a backhoe. Thousands of homes will be sold with waterfront property and access to the Bay, with one bridge to the Gulf of Mexico.

She started across the shell road and stopped abruptly in the middle of the street. She looked in both directions. There was not a car in sight. I could sit down right here and have a picnic and not be disturbed, she thought. Jerry said I should start asking questions. Where do I start, with the state, the county, or Don Buyers?

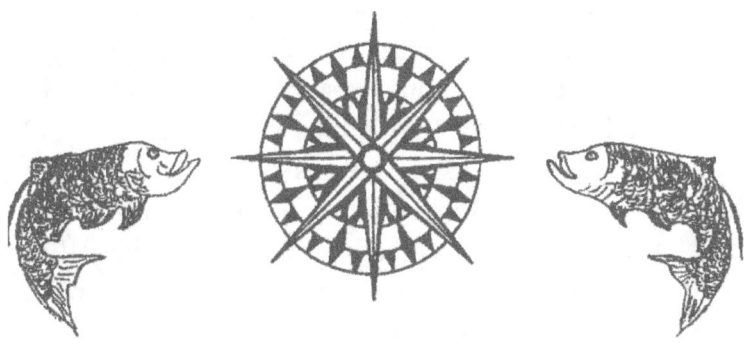

Testosterone and The Male Ego

O h, my God, just look at them," squealed one of the secretaries in the land office. Several of the other women in the office rushed to the window, where they soon joined in the appreciative sentiments of the first watcher.

A dull red pick-up truck with Georgia plates had parked in the yard and two bronzed men were busy unloading equipment. The two master stonemasons had arrived on the job site. They talked with serious drawls, chewed what had to be Red Man, and wore jeans that seemed to defy gravity. As they worked bare-chested, streams of sweat coursed down their muscular backs to disappear in deep cracks banded by the loose-hanging jeans.

"Oh, bend over, please bend over," prayed one of the women at the window."

Leroy was tall, buffed, and tanned to his waistline. He was shirtless and his muscles strained against his tight brown skin as he picked up one stone after the other. His blue jeans hung so low on his hips you could see a tuff of hair on his back just above his buttocks, where his skin was so white it looked like milk. His hair was tied back in a ponytail. Eventually the girls in the office taking in their early morning porn show could describe every inch of his unclothed body.

Ulee was shorter, and from the waist up looked like an advertisement for a Charles Atlas course. His close-cropped hair framed a face that looked as if it had been carved from one of the stones the men worked with. The severity of his features were softened by a cleft chin and twin dimples. He had another set of dimples just below his narrow waist and just above the sagging waistband of his low-slung jeans.

"What seems to be the problem, ladies?" asked Don Buyers, as he stepped out of his office. The girls quickly went back to the work, leaving an obscured view of the two workers from the windows.

The women saw Adonis and his next of kin lifting and lugging, but Buyers only saw two more cogs in his growing machine. "About time the stonemasons got here," he said. He adjusted his tie, and then went out to meet the latest members of his crew.

In the weeks to come, Leroy and Ulee proved to be star attractions. From the window in the construction office the girls could watch them set the stones on the model. They wore their blue jeans so low that every time they bent over a little of their buttocks were exposed. Consensus of opinion was they wore no underpants. It wasn't a matter of if but when their pants would slip to their knees. Every day the girls would ante up quarters and bet on when the grand unveiling would take place. Soon sexual attraction and the jackpot ensured that there would always be a pair of eyes on the industrious duo.

*****

On Monday Kate decided she was going to start asking questions. She put on a smart skirt and a tailored blouse, nothing fancy, but well designed. She even put stockings on and wore a pair of high-heeled shoes. She checked herself in the mirror: "Not bad for a women in her late thirties," she commented with a touch of bias. She made a couple of turns in front of the mirror, nodded her head in approval, and headed out the door.

Soon she drove up to the sign of the times:

DON BUYERS LAND DEVELOPMENT
GASPRILLA CONDOMINIUM PORJECT
GASPRILLA ISLAND
813-366-0000

Kate did not recognize the place. First, there was a new road with luscious landscaping and an elegant jumble of rocks with water gurgling up and out of a cunningly concealed spigot and cascading into a small pool. A beautiful model house was almost completed, save for some intricate stonework. Two men with big thighbones prominent above their low-hanging jeans were laying the finishing touches. Several other houses were in different stages of completion. Kate was impressed—the houses looked they came out of *Architectural Digest.*

She parked her car and walked up to the construction office.

"Don Buyers, please" she said to the receptionist, who happened to be standing at the window just inside the door.

"Oh, um, sure," said the dazed woman, as she tore herself away from the view of the stonemasons.

Kate turned to watch the two half-naked men laying stone and understood completely. Isabelle came up behind Kate and gave her the lowdown on Leroy and Ulee.

"...and the girls have gotten up a pool to guess when one of them will lose their pants," she babbled. "You in?"

Kate gave the duo a hard appraisal. "Give me today at 12:15," she said as she placed a quarter in the jar.

"Kate, can I come by after work today?" Isabelle asked, her smile disappearing. "I kind of want to talk to you about something."

"Sure, I'll see you later."

The Price of Crabs

"Mr. Buyers will see you now," said the receptionist, slipping past Kate to take up her post at the window.

When Kate walked into his office, Buyers stood and extended his hand. "Good to see you again, Miss Kate." She shook his hand slowly, taken aback by his presence. Don was not as she remembered him. She remembered a greasy, stuck-up, condescending man with an alligator on his shirt. But this guy was imposing; he was tall, trim, well-groomed and drop-dead good looking, with huge sparkling blue eyes like ocean waters under a bright sun. The last time she saw him was in the shop and there was an ice cream cooler between them. Now she had his full measure and had to admit, it was impressive. So this is what Isabelle sees in him.

"We've accomplished quite a bit since you were here last," he said. He offered her a seat a. "Would you like something to drink, coffee, maybe ice tea?"

"No, I am perfectly fine."

"Have you noticed how far along we are?" he bragged. "Our first model will be open in a week. We have several different models that will open in a few weeks. All roads are finished in phase one and we are beginning phase two within the next months. On the Key the roads are done and on the golf course the three holes closest to the Club House are completed. We're working on finishing the swimming the pool and the four clay tennis courts. All in all I am very pleased with the progress we are making."

He plucked a magazine off a side table and gave it to Kate. "That is the ad we're running this month. Nice picture, don't you think?"

"Yes," Kate said, beaten down by the barrage of words.

Buyers reclined in his chair until his body was almost horizontal. Then he put his legs on his desk, picked up his gold Cross-pen, and began twirling it between his fingers. "What can I help you with?"

Those are some big Florsheims, was all Kate could think, as his shining wingtips rocked her world. She felt intimidated. Kate did not expect such a confident person; he was demonstrating his power and she knew that instinctively. Between the bare-chested hunks outside and Buyers' hard sell, Kate had the same sensation she experienced the last time she visited the trailer—as if she were drowning in testosterone.

"Well," Kate hesitated a moment, then came back to herself as she remembered the reason for her visit. "When are they going to start demolition on the Shell Creek Bridge?" she blurted out. "When are they going to pave the road and how much land are you going to take from my property?"

Buyers whipped his wingtips off the desk as Kate spoke. He rose and tapped her on the shoulder.

"I want to show you the project, we can talk as we ride," he said as if he owned her. "Isabelle," he shouted, "get me the keys to the golf cart.

He did not lose a step. As Isabelle entered and handed him the keys, he gestured toward the door, then took Kate gently by the elbow and escorted her out of his office. Once outside, he led her to the golf cart and helped her into the vehicle. Kate felt like freight.

As Don drove through the development, he constantly pointed out different areas of development. He went down a new paved road and pointed to the Captiva, the Key West, the Santébell and the Pine Island, all home models that were in the process of being landscaped. He went around a cul-de-sac and into another part of the project where a retention lake was being landscaped.

"Here we are going to have duplex units; two bedrooms and two baths," he said. "The end units will have three bedrooms and three baths. In this section they will have their own pool, clubhouse, and gym." He continued talking as if Kate was not present. "Now for the best part." He drove toward the water, where the Bay narrowed and the new Intercostal Waterway flowed through. "I am very proud of this area. By the way, your son, Steven, discovered this inlet. We are going to have a quasi-marina here with a shuttle boat to the island."

Kate could see the advantages of the little marina. As she surveyed the marina she noticed Steve's boat. "Speaking of Steven, is that his boat?"

"You probably haven't spoken to Steve yet today, but I gave him a job this morning working for me this summer during school break," Don said. "We bartered for that pick-up truck he had his eye on."

"What did he barter?" Kate asked.

"The use of his boat to take people back and forth this summer until we get our ferry; I'm supplying the gas," Buyers said. "That kid of yours loves the truck and I am taking it off island this week so he can enjoy his new wheels." He continued talking, not missing a beat. "Oh, there is one more thing I need to thank you for."

"What would that be?" asked a bewildered Kate.

"I want to thank you personally for getting Isabelle interested in real estate," he said. "I am going to need a real estate agent here. Not only that, she will make a good living selling property in this development. You know women make the best Realtors."

"Isabelle a Realtor? Good for her," Kate thought. She was beginning to feel a slow burn in the pit of her stomach. I came here to ask what would happen to the Ice Cream Shop. He is rubbing my nose in how successful he has become—with the help of my family, she thought. Then he throws us a crumb, a pick-up truck, in appreciation.

"Don, I came here to ask you some questions about what is going on outside your project," she said. "I am sure you know the answers, because this development is the catalyst for all the changes."

"I haven't forgotten, I am so enthusiastic about this place I get carried away," he said. "I want to show you this wonderful place and then we can talk." He started the golf cart and scooted away. Keeping to the water's edge, he eventually pulled into a Key West-style outdoor bar and restaurant.

"Here we are." He turned off the ignition, walked around the cart and gave his hand to help Kate out of the vehicle.

"We just opened today," he said. "You will be our first guest. This place is my baby, we have an air-conditioned restaurant bar and grill and outdoor dining right on the water." He took Kate's arm again and gave her the cook's tour inside and outside. He showed the future wine cellar, outside kitchen, and barbecue. Kate was impressed. Buyers was recreating a Chicago restaurant in the middle of no man's land.

Don caught the bartender's eye, which wasn't too hard to do considering they were the only two people in the place.

"Two Bloody Marys," he said and then looked at Kate, "OK? Or would you like something else?"

"Fine," Kate answered. Why do I feel as though I am on a date? Is he trying to impress me or is he trying to distract me? They sat at a table overlooking the waterway. The bartender brought the Bloody Marys.

"It's called infrastructure, Kate."

"What?" Kate was caught off guard.

"You asked me about bridges and roads," he said. "You cannot build a development of this magnitude without infrastructure. This project will bring millions of dollars into the county and state's coffers. People will not buy a home where there is no law, no fire department, no roads, and no hospitals." He took a sip of his drink.

"I want to know about the Shell Creek Bridge, the road in front of my property."

"Kate, you already know that Shell Creek Bridge is going to be replaced along with Turtle Creek Bridge, and several other bridges in the area," he said. "You have the only commercial enterprise between the two bridges. The county and state will not put in a one-way bridge because it's not cost effective.

"The surveyors start next week surveying. I'd say in two months they start construction. First they dig up the road, do the earthmoving, put in sewers, demolish the bridges, and while they are doing the demolition a new road will be built from RT 775 to RT 776. It'll be a connector road. North of Shell Creek the county is already building a sub-station that will hold the sheriff's office, board of health and county offices in Charlotte County. Sarasota County has building plans too. You can go to the planning offices of both counties and they will have the information you need."

"What's going on across the street, where Bob's Bait House used to be?" Kate asked. "Did you have something to do with that sale of property?"

"I did not buy that property, the state did. You know, that is a beautiful piece of land."

"How did the state know about it?"

"Aerial photography," Buyers said, pleased with himself. "I had a friend from Chicago take photos of the whole area. I thought the state would be interested in a future public boat ramp and a small park. It actually fits the requirement for green space that the state has in place." He finished his drink, ordered another one, and then placed an order for lunch. Kate had no choice in the lunch order; it seemed it was all previously prearranged.

She sat there watching the pelicans dive for fish. "Who demanded all this infrastructure?"

"I did," he said, as if she had asked a stupid question.

Kate looked at Don, "Why would the state or county

or both go through all this expense for roads, bridges, public boat ramps, parks, sheriff's station, fire department and county offices here in this small area of Shell Creek with only a few hundred people?"

"Because they're getting ready for the future." Don said.

Kate sat quietly looking out the window, watching the pelicans while lunch was served. Her plate contained a beautiful baked grouper with a key lime sauce, wild rice, and steamed vegetables.

"How many people do you estimate will move here?" Kate asked.

"Let me see, the figure is 2.1 persons per household; some households will be seasonal, others will be full time residents. The state estimates an increase between 150,000 and 200,000 per zip code."

Kate stopped eating, her fork mid-air. "You've got to be kidding?" Then another thought crossed her mind. "You don't own that much land... or do you?"

"Well, I own most of the land west of the road, I have options on the land east of the road, and I own land surrounding the future boat ramp and park," he said. "I have approved Plan Unit Development plans for the land; if I decide that I want out of the building business. I'll just sell off the land to a new developer." Don gave a confident grin. "Either way the die has been cast."

Where have I heard that statement before? Kate thought. "So the surveyors are starting next week to place stakes for the road and the new bridge," Kate asked. "The road will remain open 'til they start to demolish the bridge. Then the road will be closed to traffic both ways for approximately two years. Is that correct?"

"That is about right," Don said, patting his lips with his napkin. "You will be out of business for about two years. If you can hang on that long and reopen, you'll have three times as many customers... if you can hang on that long."

Kate's mind raced. Her heart seemed to match the same pace, pounding in her chest like a trip-hammer. She knew that they were situated between two counties, Sarasota and Charlotte, which meant that all Buyers' projections could be doubled if he played the two governments off against each other. And in their blindness to raise their tax bases, neither government would consider the impact of their greed. That meant there could be as many as 100,000 to 300,000 additional residents. Every square inch of land would have a house, condo, duplex, clubhouse, gym, country club, roads, commercial buildings, and nothing left after Buyers and other developers were through.

Kate felt sick to her stomach. "Can we go?" she asked politely. "I've been away too long. I left the 'GONE FISHING' sign on the door and I need to get back."

"Sure." Don put his napkin down beside his plate and motioned to the waiter that they were leaving. They left the restaurant, got into the golf cart, and headed back to the office. Don continued his lecture as Kate began to sweat. She looked up and shaded her eyes as the early afternoon sun hammered the hard-packed, gleaming pathway of crushed shells like a high-impact drill.

"You developers clear cut the land and don't leave a tree standing," she fumed. "What you plant does not replace what has been taken away—a cute palm tree for a live oak."

The trees and greenery that gave shade and kept things cool are ripped out and the sun pours down on pavements, road, and rooftops, she thought, causing the ambient temperature to rise. You build roads and then landscape but your high-rise buildings and condos block the ocean breeze. She shook her head.

"It's as if you purposely want to mess up paradise," Kate said.

"Well, that's one way to look at it," Buyers said airily, as if Kate had merely remarked on the weather. "I'm no scientist, and by the way, neither are you, so that's just your opinion."

"But, Don," Kate said, "It's almost as if you're poisoning your new residents."

"What?" Buyers asked, stopping the cart and truly looking at Kate. "What did you say?"

"Look at that sun," Kate said, as they sat beneath the boiling orb. "Too much sun. You've ripped up the oaks that were here and replaced them with these palm trees to make paradise look like your idea of paradise. But they don't provide any shade. So all that sun causes cancer. And what about the water, all those people flushing toilets, watering lawns, using fertilizers, pesticides, and fungicides? Run-off drains into the creeks, then into Gulf of Mexico and we have major pollution.

For a moment, Buyers sat stunned, sweat glistening on his high forehead. He turned to Kate. "Last time I looked, you ran an ice cream shop, not a science lab," he sneered. Then, with slow, deliberate moves, he turned the key in the ignition, pushed down on the gas, and began driving the golf cart back to his office.

When they got back to construction office, after a trip made in silence, Buyers said, "There is one more thing I want to thank you for."

"What would that be?" Kate asked.

"Remember the first time we met, what you said to me?" Buyers asked, leaning close.

"I said a lot of things," Kate replied.

Buyers gave a vile grin. "If you hadn't said that I had an alligator mouth with a canary ass, I would not be here today. You see, Kate, you are the catalyst for all this development, not me. I am simply proving you wrong."

"Well, consider me wrong," Kate snapped back, "'cause you're making a lot of shit for one sorry-ass alligator." She hopped off the cart. "Thank you for lunch, it was very interesting. I don't want to come in to see your plot plans—or your etchings!" She turned and left.

Yes, she looked good strutting to the car in her nice skirt and sexy blouse, with chest thrust out and head up high. But inside, behind the haughtiness, the world had just come apart for Kate. The pain in the pit of her stomach was there and would be there for a long time. If she could vomit she probably would feel better. But she would not give Buyers the satisfaction of seeing her retch.

She drove home at a snail's crawl. When she pulled into her drive she noticed the 'GONE FISHING' sign was gone. Somehow it didn't matter anymore, nothing mattered.

Philip greeted Kate at the door. "Hi, mom. I took over while you were playing hooky. We were busy for a while; I could have used some help."

She had to smile. Kids were great and right now, she needed a smile. "Thanks, honey, I was gone longer than I should have. You can go now; I'll be here for the rest of the day."

''OK, see you later," Philip said, flying out the door, "I'll be back for supper."

Kate slumped in the closest chair and put her face into her hands. She kept running the conversation over and over again. Did I create this situation with my remark? I was just being a smart ass. I can't take back what I said; who said words are things, what a profound statement. Even if I apologized nothing would change. But another voice told her she couldn't turn back the tide, even if she did apologize, because Buyers is on a mission to prove his manhood.

Isabelle came rushing into the ice cream shop.

"Kate, Kate, guess what? You won, you won."

Kate was not happy to see Isabelle; she represented the devil's whore. Kate was furious; Isabelle's boss had just made her feel like a powerless fool.

"Won what, Isabelle?" Kate barely lifted her head from her hands.

"The Leroy-Ulee pool," the blond exclaimed. "At exactly at 12:15, Ulee bent over to lift a large stone," Isabelle was so excited she could barely speck fast enough. "When his blue jeans fell down to his knees; he didn't even bother to pull up his pants, He just turned around and saluted. Then he looked over at us girls in the office staring at him and laughed his head off." Isabelle shook the jar up and down and then placed the jar on the table next to Kate. "Here are your winnings."

Kate lifted her head slowly. She deliberately pushed the jar off the table. It shattered. Glass and quarters scattered all over the floor "I don't want any of this Judas money."

Isabelle stood shocked. "What are you talking about?

"I am talking about you and your boss. How can you kiss him let alone fuck him. He is the serpent in the Garden of Eden. He is the most deceptive person I have ever known."

Shocked and dismayed, Isabelle started to cry. She ran from the shop.

Shit runs downhill, Kate thought as she instantly regretted taking out her anger on Don Buyers' girlfriend.

A few seconds later, Jerry entered the store. Hard on his heels was Philip.

"What's all that noise?" the boy asked. "Oh, hey Jerry." He looked at the glass and money on the floor and his eyes grew wide. "Mom, I will sweep up the mess if I can keep the money, l can use the quarters, for pinball."

"Pinball?" Kate looked at her younger son, and then laughed. "So, it's down to pinball, I guess that's, what matters. Have fun."

She turned to Jerry and asked, "Do you know where Isabelle lives?"

Jerry nodded his head.

"Jerry, can you take me there, I need to apologize to her."

"Apologize for what, Kate?"

"I'll explain everything on the way over there," Kate said. "Okay Philip, please sweep that up, and would you mind the store for a an hour?"

His eyes gleaming with silver, Philip rapidly agreed.

On their way to Isabelle's villa Kate told Jerry about her conversation with Don. She railed about his superior attitude and his plans to transform the area. The worst part, she said, was how Buyers had co-opted her own family. Then she told Jerry about Buyers thanking her for steering Isabelle to real estate school.

"The final insult was when he thanked me for calling him an alligator mouth with a canary asshole, Jerry," she said. "He thanked me and said because of that comment he had to prove me wrong."

Jerry just kept on driving and did not make a comment. His silence unnerved Kate.

"Jerry did you understand what I was saying?"

"He would have made a good boxer," Jerry said. He lured you right into a corner and then gave you the sucker punch right into the gut."

"What do you mean?"

"Kate, Don would have found that cut in the mangroves sooner or later, especially since he has access to aerial photography. Steven only showed him the cut because he wanted to show off his knowledge of the water. If Don gives him the truck it's because he can afford to give the truck away. It may be a crumb to him but to Steve it is the world. I would not say word to Steve, let him have his dream."

Kate fumed, and made as if to speak, but Isabelle's villa loomed just ahead. They pulled up and Jerry turned off the engine.

"I'll wait here while you apologize to Isabelle," Jerry said.

Kate slid out of the car and walked up to the front door and rang the doorbell. There was no answer and she rang again.

"Isabelle, are you there?" She saw a curtain flutter, as if someone had peeked to see who was at the door. "It's Kate, I came to apologize. I am so sorry for what said, it was cruel, mean, and hateful. I didn't mean to strike out at you; it was Don that made me so angry." Kate started to cry. The door still remained close.

In the car on the way back to the ice cream shop, Kate said. "Who would have thought that my whole life would change because of my big mouth? Whatever possessed me to criticize him?"

"Well, Kate, you may have a big mouth," Jerry said.

"What?" Now Kate was furious all over again. She had poured out her heart to Jerry, and the best he could do was criticize her.

"Whatever, I wish I had never said anything. If I

could take back those words I would in a heartbeat." Kate sobbed, as she left Jerry's car.

"Kate, there is no life without regrets." Jerry said.

"You're being a philosopher again."

"No, I just had a lot of counseling," he said. "Buck up, sister," the ex-boxer said. "You can take a punch, so go with it. For some unknown reason you challenged him."

He idled the engine as he waited for Kate to get out of his vehicle. "Now I'm going to try to patch things with Isabelle, if she's ready to talk." He smiled at Kate and drove away.

"So, Jerry, you too have seen the belly of the snake," Kate said as he drove away.

No sooner did Jerry leave then a green 1956 Chevy pick-up came bouncing into the driveway. Talk about adding insult to injury, Kate thought. Steven vigorously waved his arm out the window and indicated his new wheels. Kate forced a smile and walked to greet her son.

"Isn't this a beautiful truck?"

"You look good behind the wheel." Kate smiled

"I'm going to paint it and fix it up a little.

"I think I would varnish the wooden bed to its original color and put a couple coats of polyurethane on top." Kate suggested. Her boy's enthusiasm was contagious; it helped lift her out of her feelings of failure.

"Hey, that is a good idea."

"Has your brother seen your truck yet?"

"No."

"Go show him and take him for a ride, have fun."

"I think we'll take a run down to Jerry's and show off the truck, I bet he'll have some good ideas." Steve said as he ran into the house to get his bother.

Leroy & Ulee

*L*eroy and Ulee had just finished the stonework on the models. They were currently working on a private residence. The owners had selected blue and grey river rock that had to be imported from Tennessee at an exorbitant cost. It was only eight o'clock in the morning. The stonemasons had their T-shirts off and they exuded an abundance of male testosterone with their suntans and bulging muscles covered in sweat.

The owner of the house, a Mrs. Powers from Nantucket, came by to check on the progress of her home. She was a good-looking woman, tall, slender, and about forty years old. She wore white linen slacks, a navy and white cotton nautical sweater, gold hoop earrings, and a heavy gold chain bracelet. She lived on the Cliffs of Nantucket, which bespoke millions. She was rigid and haughty with a New England accent and smelled of 'Chanel No.5.'

When Don Buyers spotted her he rushed out of his office to greet her and extol the progress of her new home. He was more than pleased to act as host and guide her through her house. As Don and Mrs. Powers walked the project, they spotted Leroy and Ulee. The stonemasons also saw Buyers and Mrs. Powers.

Leroy went to his cooler and pulled out a beer. He popped the lid and took a long swig; his eyes never left Mrs. Powers. Ulee, following suit, took a pack of cigarettes from the pocket of his shirt, which lay on a pile of stones. He lit his cigarette and took a long deep inhale. He let out the smoke through his mouth and inhaled the smoke again through his nose and exhaled through his mouth.

"Hi, guys," Buyers, said as he approached the men. But before he could get anything else out of his mouth, Leroy and Mrs. Powers locked eyes. Leroy watched her walk and he eyed her body with unmistakable lust from head to toe and then from toe to head. He was so obvious that her nipples turned hard under her sweater. He noticed her reaction and stared at her hardened nipples. Leroy lifted his beer, took another swig, and then he let out the most audible belch ever heard.

"Humph," Mrs. Powers said in disgust. She turned

around and walked back to the office.

"You guys pack up your tools and be in my office in five minutes," Don said. He followed Mrs. Powers back to the office.

Once he got back to the office he snapped at the staff. "There will be no more pools; take that jar of quarters and do something constructive with the money," he told the girls in the office. "Isabelle get Jim right now." Don was seething at the gills. He apologized to Mrs. Powers and gave her a discount on her stonework to save the contract on her house. As he ushered her out of the office, she blanched. Leroy and Ulee stopped and stared at her as she scuttled around them and made for her car. Then the two entered Don's office.

"You're fired, here are your paychecks and I do not want to see you around here anymore," he barked.

"That ain't what we get paid." Leroy said. Jim came into the office and was quickly filled in as to what had just transpired.

"That ain't what we get paid." Leroy said again.

Jim picked up the check and told Leroy and Ulee in a no-nonsense tone of voice. "Take this check and cash it at the bank and do not make any more waves, do you UNDERSTAND?" Both guys looked at Jim, then turned away. They slowly walked out of the office with Jim following behind them. Don could see Jim talking to them. Finally Leroy and Ulee got in their pick-up truck and drove away.

Jim heard an earful when he returned to the office.

"Those two rednecks almost cost me a $400,000

sale," he yelled. "And I lost a cut of that just to keep my client satisfied." Buyers laid down the new protocol. "There will never be anyone running around this project without a shirt again. I don't care if it is a hundred-and-ten in the shade and the heat index is two hundred. From now on, there is a dress code if I have to buy the shirts myself. Is that understood?"

Jim nodded, but he didn't say a word. He turned to leave.

"One more thing; there will be no beer on this project, not even after work," he thundered. "Is that understood?"

Jim did not turn or stop, he just left the office.

Enter the Law

*T*he fishermen had just left after their morning coffee and Kate was doing prep work for the day when the bell on the door jingled. She looked up to see a deputy in his official uniform.

"Anything wrong?" Kate asked in surprise.

"No, I just came by to introduce myself."

"I have two teenage boys and when I see the law I automatically think there is something wrong," she laughed. "Are you from around here?"

The officer laughed and nodded his head. "No, I was just stationed here, just up the road in the new sheriff's office. I'm Andy Struhart, deputy with the Charlotte County Sheriff's Department." He reached out to shake Kate's hand. She wiped her hand on her apron and then took his.

"I'm Kate Callahan, nice to meet you. Would you like some coffee or ice cream?"

"Maybe some ice cream. I know it's early in the day, but I have a hankering for ice cream."

"Okay, what flavor?

"Chocolate Almond."

While Kate scooped the ice cream into a dish, she eyed the officer. He was medium built, about five feet eleven inches. He looked strong, young, and handsome. He was in complete uniform, gun, flak jack, radio, and God knows what else hanging from his belt. He noticed Kate staring at him.

"Standard work clothes, you might say."

"You look so impressive. I'm not used to seeing the law down here. We really don't have any crime per se."

"I know that," he said. "I'm just making friendly calls today. Here is my card with the emergency phone number, office number, and my private number just in case." He pointed to Kate's telephone. "I would put this above your phone."

Kate was surprised that he had cased the shop and spotted the phone on the wall.

"My family's moving in this weekend," he said, lightening the tension.

"So you're married. Have any children?

"Yes, a daughter, and one on the way."

Kate poured herself a cup of coffee and relaxed.

"Where're you from?"

"Born and raised in Florida, went to school at Florida State in Tallahassee"

"So you're from the Panhandle?"

"Apalachicola, to be exact."

"Great, you have some of the most beautiful beaches up there. Welcome to Shell Creek. Hope you like it here. We're a small community and you won't find much crime here."

"That is okay by me," he said. "I'd rather be a friendly member of the community than a watchdog. What do I owe you for the ice cream?"

"It is on the house."

"No favors. My family will always pay for everything. Thank you again."

He paid and left. Kate shook her head. We have the law now. That damn Don Buyers. He brings in the law where there's no crime, but now there will be crime because that is their business, to fine lawbreakers. Shit, she thought, then comes the churches here to find strife because nobody can be happy in paradise, and then comes the banks and the moneychangers. As she thought, she wiped harder at the condensation on the coolers, working out her anger on the omnipresent moisture that beaded up on the double panes of glass.

The next day the buzz was the new deputy sheriff. The fishermen were doing nothing but speculating why he was here. Kate was hardy listening; her mind was somewhere else. I don't mind the law's presence because in six months I'll be somewhere else, she thought, where I don't know.

"Kate."

"Yes," a startled Kate answered, coming back to the present

"Did he say anything else or did he ask any questions?" asked Roger

"Actually no, I thought he was a quite pleasant; he is a nice looking young man with a family," she said.

The fishermen were huddled around the table and talking in a conspiratorial tone.

"What are you boys conjuring about?'

Dwayne spoke up. "Last week, east of here, somewhere around El Jobean, the sheriff's department found an airplane full of drugs."

"What?" Kate's mouth fell open.

"Yeah, they found a single-engine plane that landed on a deserted road," Chappie said. The pilot was gone. He ran, accordin' to the deputy. They're tryin' to track down the owner of the plane and the pilot."

"The pilot ran away, but the FBI is checking the ownership of the plane," Roger said.

"Maybe that's why the law is here," Harold chimed in.

"Why didn't you guys mention this before?" Kate asked.

"Because you have too much on your plate right now, and we didn't want to worry you," Roger said.

"Kate, did you know the guy who used to own this building would bring in drugs?" Dwayne asked. "They would pull up to your dock, unload and Cagey Ernie would say he knew nothing about anything."

"I didn't realize we had a drug problem here," Kate said.

"We don't," Roger said. "Just every once in a while you hear a story, someone tryin' to make easy money. Come on boys, the fish are singin'" he said. The men all stood at the same time and left.

Gasparilla Beacon - 1979

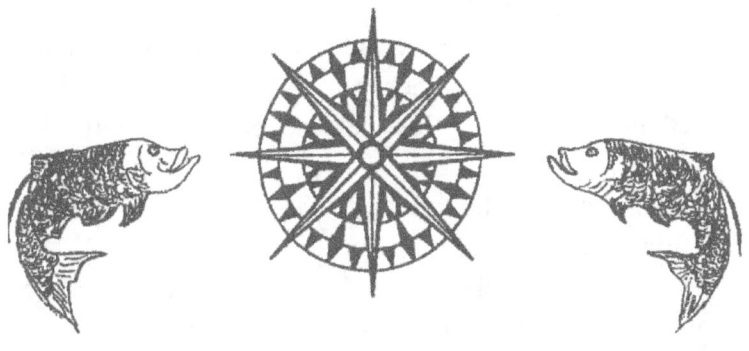

The Tarpon Tournament

A sudden rap at the door startled her. It was late; the Ice Cream Shop had closed hours ago. Kate had just finished doing inventory, and was giving the coolers one last wipe before calling it quits.

She looked up. Chappie stood outside the door, shining in the moonlight because of his usual outfit of white painter's pants and equally white T-shirt.

"What are you up to this time of night?" Kate asked as she opened the door.

"Hey, you know you been talkin' 'bout wantin' ta do

some tarpon fishin'?" Chappie asked without even a greeting. He was in a hurry.

"Yes?"

"Well, get a move on," Chappie said gesturing with his hands. "We done had a cancellation tonight and I got a spot open on my boat."

Either wipe down the coolers or go tarpon fishing? For Kate, it was a no-brainer.

"Okay," she said. "Just let me check in with the boys."

"Meet me at the boat dock," Chappie said, giving her directions even as he climbed back into his jeep.

On the way to the dock Kate stopped at the Crab Lady's place and bought two dozen dollar crabs.

"Going for the fish of kings?" asked the Crab Lady, a wry grin on her face as she snipped pincers.

"What? Oh, tarpon fishing." Kate answered. For some reason she felt embarrassed. Tarpon fishing was developed as a sport for the wealthy. Chappie and captains like him chartered their boats at premium rates to tarpon tournament clients. If they pulled in a record tarpon the captain stood to make a big tip.

"No worries," the Crab Lady said, "I'm just pulling your leg. Chappie's a good captain— I'm surprised that two men cancelled on him. And he's a good man for finding tarpon."

As she spoke, the boy shambled out from behind the house. He was holding his bleeding left hand He ran toward the Crab Lady, who dropped what she was doing and pulled him close.

"You know what to do," she said, looking back over her shoulder at Kate and motioning to the crabs. "I have to…"

"I'll be fine, go ahead and take care of him…is there anything you need?" Kate asked, as she gathered the crabs. But the boy and the Crab Lady were already moving away, as the woman steered him toward the house.

When Kate got to the boat dock she spotted Jim's red mane. He was helping Chappie get everyone settled. The two paying customers were already strapped into the sissy chairs waiting to go.

"I'm sorry I'm late," Kate said. "I had to get these." She held up the pail of crabs. Jim took them from her and put them in the bait well.

"We already have plenty of bait," Jim said by way of greeting her. The paying customers were anxious to get going. Jim went into the cockpit with Chappie and Kate followed. Chappie's boat was well equipped with electronics; he had radar, ship to shore radio, depth finder, and a fish finder. He proudly described each feature to Kate as he steered toward Gasparilla Pass.

Several boats silhouetted against the moonlit water bobbed and rose in the swell as they entered the pass.

"Well, gentleman," Jim said to the paying customers, "We have a full moon, summer solstice and an outgoing tide. This is a perfect night to catch a tarpon." Both men, who according to Chappie had paid through the nose for the opportunity to be in tonight's tournament, were buoyed by Jim's announcement. He baited each of their rods with a dollar crab and cast their lines out, showing them how to troll behind the boat. They shrugged him off, claiming they already knew how to do that.

Chappie started a slow run through the pass and then made a gentle turn to reenter the pass.

"May I have a rod?" Kate asked, surprised by her own boldness.

"Here," Jim smirked. "Do you know how to bait a rod?'

Kate nodded. Remembering the Crab Lady's technique, Kate reached into the bait well and took out a dollar crab. She removed the pincher, drilled a hole in the shell, and baited her hook.

"Wait a minute," Jim said as she prepared to cast. He took the rod and moved her away from the paying customers. "These guys paid big money for a shot, we can't have you fouling their lines," he growled.

"So what am I, chopped liver?" Kate responded.

"Whatever."

A few of the fishermen on the other boats had a fish on their lines, which made the two tournament guys on board antsy. Their mood didn't improve when Kate suddenly got a bite. Her rod bent double as the huge fish strained to escape. His weight pulled Kate into the railing. Jim grabbed her rod and pulled. Then he made a slicing motion to Chappie, who cut the line.

"You had a large fish, probably a Jew fish, and we don't have the time for that," Jim said.

Kate noticed that his eyes slid away from hers as he talked. Liar, she thought, but decided to be quiet. After all, she wasn't a paying customer. As Chappie meandered up and down the pass, Kate's temper cooled. The monotony of the trawling settled her nerves, and she began to enjoy the exhilarating feeling of drifting along in the moonlight.

However, the two clients on board weren't as calm. Other fishermen in other boats kept on getting bites. When the tarpon in the water started to roll, they came to the surface. Kate marveled as she watched them roll over and over in the moonlight. Both of Chappie's customers grew more jealous by the minute as they watched their rivals pull tarpon from the Gulf. Finally even Chappie decided enough was enough.

"Gentlemen, I'm going to make one more pass, then I'm going to have to take this old vessel home," he said. Kate glanced at her watch; it was almost 11. What the hell? She put a fresh dollar crab on her line and threw the rest of them overboard. Out of the corner of her eye she saw Jim headed her way so she cast her line before he could grab her rod.

He scowled; Kate stuck out her tongue and concentrated on her fishing. Suddenly she felt a powerful jerk on her line. She was pulled off her seat and almost over the gunnels. Jim grabbed Kate around the waist. She sat on the bait-well and braced her legs on the gunnels, put the rod between her legs, and hunkered down for a fight.

"Set the hook," shouted Chappie.

"I did," Kate screamed, struggling with the bent pole.

Jim stood so close she could feel his breath against her neck. He was ready to grab her in case the tarpon pull her over board. She tried to squirm away; as she did so the line went slack.

"I lost him," Kate sighed.

Jim took the rod from her hands and gave it a sharp tug. Suddenly the tarpon fought back, starting a run for freedom.

"Ha-ha, that sucker's still there," Jim, crowed. Kate's feelings soared. As she reached for her rod, Jim turned and handed it to one of the paying customers.

"Here," he said, "see how a tarpon feels on your line," The man leaned into it, flexing as if the fish were his from the start of the fight.

"That's my fish and I want to bring it in," Kate shouted, "I can do this, it's my fish." She felt like a two-year-old whining about a toy, but she stood her ground. Jim gave her back the rod, but assumed his too-close position behind her.

Soon her arms, back and legs were crying for relief. But she held on. I am woman; watch me fish, she screamed silently as she felt the power of the fish course through her. The line went slack for a moment and she used the momentum to hurl an elbow back into Jim's midsection.

"Ooof," he yelped.

"Give me room," Kate hissed at him. Jim gave a rueful grin and backed up out of her personal space.

Then the tarpon leaped out of the water. He went high, about twenty-thirty feet above the water, and he danced on his tail against the full moon. It was the most beautiful scene Kate had ever seen. He was covered in phosphorous, like the glow Kate remembered from her night fishing with Jerry on Shell Creek. He rolled as he leaped, an enormous glittering fish against the silvery moon of the summer solstice. Then he fell back in the water. He leaped once more, but after his magnificent jump he was exhausted. From then on it was a downhill battle as Kate slowly pulled him in.

He jumped one last time but not as high. Kate wished for a moment that Chappie had cut this line and not the earlier one. She reeled it to the side of the boat and Jim asked. "What do you want to do with this fish?"

"I want to keep him," Kate answered. The paying customers bit back their disappointment and congratulated her. But for some reason, Kate wasn't as proud as she thought she would be.

After taking the record-breaking tarpon down to The Fishery to be place it on ice, Kate left Chappie and Jim and drove home alone. She fell into bed, her body one giant bruise, and overslept the alarm clock the next day.

Stephen and Philip's bantering awakened her. She glanced at the clock, then leaped out of bed and rushed to get ready for business.

As she pushed the boys out the door on the way to school, Kate saw the fishermen approaching.

Soon they were in their favorite seats in the Ice Cream Shop, guzzling coffee and giving her mischievous looks.

Kate was dreaming how she was going to mount the tarpon and was about to tell the fishing buddies about her episode last night. When---

"You really brought that fish in yourself last night?" asked Harold.

Kate felted indignant that Harold should ask that question. So she rolled up her sleeves and showed them the black and blue marks from the fight on her forearms. They all gasped.

"How big was it?" Roger asked.

"He weighed a hundred-and-twenty pounds and was five feet three inches. If I were in the tournament I would have won. He was the biggest catch of the day. And the biggest catch of my life."

"Now, was that big fish worth getting Chappie damn near killed?" Dwayne asked. The other two fishermen roared with laughter.

"Chappie?" Kate was embarrassed. She hadn't even noticed that Chappie was absent from the breakfast club. "What happened to Chappie?"

"He's in Venice General Hospital," Roger said, "Mary Ellen shot him full of salt pellets."

"What? You've got to be kidding." Kate shook her head. "Why?"

"Because he took you tarpon fishing and he never took her," Roger said. "Then you went and caught the winning fish, so Chappie didn't even get a tip—you cost her money!"

"He'll be in the hospital for a couple of days," Dwayne said.

"Did Mary Ellen get charged with anything?" Kate asked.

Chappie told the law he had been cleaning his gun,

Dwayne explained, and forgot both barrels were loaded with salt pellets. "Of course, no one cleans a gun at two o'clock in the mornin," Dwayne cackled.

"Are you sure he is okay?" Kate asked.

"Kate we're just teasing you," Roger said, grinning broadly. "That was the shot that broke the camel's back."

What? Kate thought.

"That's right, Harold said. "They gettin' married next week," Chappie said, 'Any woman love me that much, I have to marry.'"

"Between getting' shot an' proposin' Chappie is milkin the situation for all its worth," Roger said. "It's 'honey get me this and honey get me that, now you have to take care of me, I am wounded.'"

"Roger, I feel so bad, was I suppose to tip Chappie?"

"Kate, no we are just teasin' you. Chappie will be fine and he wanted to take you tarpon fishin' as a thank you for all the free breakfasts you have served us.

SW Tip of Boca Grande - circa 1981

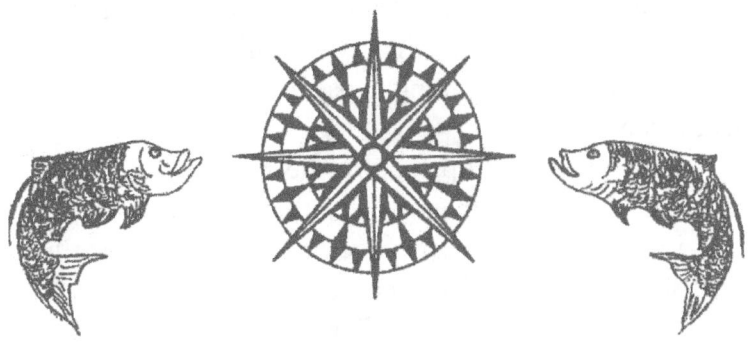

The No Name Storm

*T*hat night a storm brewed in the Gulf. It started to rain and then poured, and it became torrential. The wind began to howl. Kate turned on the radio for the latest weather forecast. The announcer warned of a tropical storm, but not much more, and urged listeners not to worry.

But the weather soon became worrisome. The atmospheric pressure dropped. Kate had a headache and could feel the pressure in her ears. Philip's ears popped. Then, at five o'clock in the afternoon, it grew as dark as midnight. Kate turned the radio on again. All she heard was static.

"This reminds me of when I was a kid in Ohio and we had tornadoes," Kate said to Philip. "Let's go outside and pick up what we can before the storm hits."

They rummaged around outside, then checked Kate's boat to make sure the lines were good and tight. By the time they finished, the wind was really blowing hard. Palm fronds were breaking loose from trees that were leaning sideways.

"Let's get in, Philip, before the blow starts." Once inside they changed their wet clothes Steven, who had been in bed with what the doctor said was bronchitis, came staggering out of his bedroom.

"I gotta check on my boat," he muttered.

"You're not going anywhere." Kate said. But she knew how much his boat meant to him. "Phil and I will check on it, honey."

"Yeah, I'll go, Mom," Philip said.

"Turn on the bilge, it will automatically get rid of the water and check the lines," Steven said.

"Sure."

"Steven, go back to bed, we know what to do." Kate said.

"Aw, Mom."

Philip grabbed a five-gallon bucket and off they went. As they drove south on Route 776 the storm intensified. Palm fronds and tree branches lay across the road, which was flooded in places. The wind blew the car first one way and then another. Kate had a hard time keeping it on the road. The rain stopped and the wind died down as she turned into the marina where Steve kept his boat. She parked the car next to the dock. Kate grabbed the bucket and then she and Philip headed down to the boat.

The boat was already filled with water up to its gunnels. Phil took off his shoes and socks and handed them to Kate. He jumped into the boat and searched for the bilge under the water. But it was waterlogged and worthless. The boat was unstable with water slowly coming over the stern. As Phil moved around, one of the lines snapped and the boat whipped from side to side. Kate started to get in.

"No, Mom," Philip yelled. "You get in and we'll sink. Hand me that bucket and go get the rope I put in the truck, hurry."

Phil bailed like a madman as Kate ran to the car. When she returned with the rope, Philip leaped out of the boat. He had bailed out about an inch of water.

"You start bailing," he shouted, "you weigh less than I do "I'm going to cross tie the boat to the other dock." He grabbed the rope from Kate's hands; he lashed it to a loop on the bow of the boat, and then secured it to a cleat on the piling near the starboard side. He did the same on the boat's port side.

All the while Kate bailed, but her efforts appeared futile. The wind blew so hard the rain came at her sideways; she could barely see or hear as the rained blasted her like needles.

Philip secured the bow and scrambled to tie down the stern. After doing so, he shouted at his mother.

"Mom, take everything out of the boat," he screamed

over the roar of the wind. "We'll put everything in the back seat of your car. I'll take the motor off the boat and take it home too."

It took Kate several trips back and forth to the car, with the wind slashing her face and pushing her backwards, to carry tackle box, life preservers, fishing rods, cooler, toolbox, flashlights, and everything else. She was soon soaked to the bone and chilly; the rain had turned cold. On her final trip, the wind was so strong that it pushed Kate sideways. She fell into the boat. She rose to her knees and started bailing again. She had to brace herself against the gunnels.

Philip took off the 25 hp engine and put it on the dock. He carried the motor to the car and placed it in the truck. He came back and loosened the lines. The tide was coming fast and he didn't want the tide to lodge the boat under the dock.

"Mom," he screamed against the wind, "let's go. We can't do anymore. Let's go before we get swept away." Kate could not hear him but she saw him waving his arms. She tried to get out of the boat, but the wind and rain pushed her back down. Philip ran over and gave her his hand, but the waves kept tossing the boat around. Kate knew the only way out was to crawl, not try to stand. Philip grabbed her under her arm and Kate wrapped her other arm around the piling once she had her knee on the dock, Philip helped her up and she held on tight to the pilling.

They braced themselves against the force of the wind and made it back to the car. They could not open the door on the windward side of the car, so Kate had to crawl into the passenger side and then cross over once they were inside. When they got back to the ice cream shop Kate parked on the lee side of the building. Kate went to check on Steve, but he wasn't there.

"Steven," Kate yelled.

When Philip came inside he said, "Steve's bailing out your boat."

"No, he can't be doing that."

"Well he is. Mom, go get a couple buckets and meet us at the boat dock. I'm going to help him."

Phil ran outside. Suddenly the lights went out.

"Oh, no," Kate yelled. She went into the Ice Cream Shop and checked the temperature in the coolers. "I'm okay if the lights are off for no more than three hours, after that I'll lose all the ice cream. She opened the freezer and took a quick count of the five-gallon containers of ice cream she had stored. She counted ten.

"Oh God, let the lights come back on." Kate said.

Just as Kate headed back out into the storm, a pick-up truck pulled into the parking lot. What is that guy looking for, she thought. Not ice cream?

"Hey Lady, I thought I would come and check on you," the driver shouted.

Kate let out a great sigh of relief, it was Jerry.

"The kids are out back trying to save my boat."

He held Kate's arm as they fought the wind. The buckets she had picked up acted like sails, Kate hung on for dear life.

Steven and Philip were trying to retrieve the boat and

let out the lines. Kate had tied her boat up short to the dock, unaware of the coming storm. When storm surge came the bow got caught under the dock and filled up with water. It was almost capsized. Phil and Kate bailed and Steve and Jerry retied the boat loose enough to float with the rise of the water. But Kate's boat motor was too big and heavy to take off in the middle of a storm.

"If it sinks so what?" Kate yelled. "Better than us getting hurt trying to save a boat. Let's get inside."

With Jerry in the lead breaking the wind for all of them, they went into the house single file and holding each other's hand.

Once inside they all changed into dry clothes. Philip led Jerry into his room and gave him some jeans and a sweatshirt. Steven had the chills even though he was running a fever. Kate gave him his medicine. They had no electricity so Kate could not make coffee or hot tea, or a hot toddy for Steven. So she gave him a shot of whisky and a vapor rub on his chest and then sent him to bed under a lot of covers.

"You little fool," she said, kissing him as he tried to squirm away.

The wind kept up for hours. The windows rattled. The debris from Bob's late Bait House swept across the road. It hit the front windows and started to pile up against the shop and house. Kate saw broken oak tree limbs, palm fronds, papers, and soda cans in the yard. But the scariest sight was the pine needles blown with such force they were embedded in the wooden doorframe.

The Price of Crabs

The high tide surged and the water flooded over the banks of Shell Creek. It ran across the road, drained into the old Bait House property, and emptied into the lagoon on the other side of the road.

The storm ended as fast as it came. The wind calmed down and the rain stopped, but the lights never came on. All the ice cream in the coolers and freezer melted, creating a river of goo.

Jerry left when the rain stopped. "I'll be back in the morning to help clean up," he promised.

Steven slept well. At eleven o'clock an exhausted Kate went to bed.

The next morning Steven was worse so Kate took Steve to Venice Memorial Hospital where he was admitted with pneumonia. Philip went to check on Steven's boat, which rode out the storm. Soon he was ferrying men over to the island. The conversation was about the storm, the damages, and the cleanup. Roger said folks were calling it "The No Name Storm," because it formed at the last minute without warning. It surprised everyone. The construction site was swept clean of everything that was lighter than cinder blocks. But other than that everything looked the same.

Stump Pass - 1970's

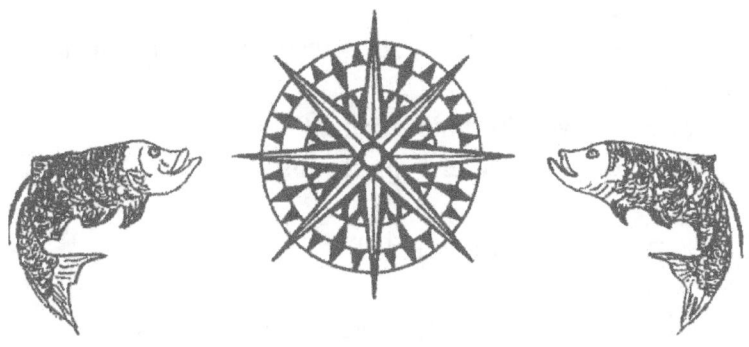

Did He Come On Level

*P*hilip followed the men to the job site. He replaced Steven as the guy who ferried the men to work. Phil would talk to Roger, ask a lot of questions, and act as if he were a straw boss. As he wandered around the construction site he saw Jim with a plumb line and level checking a recently laid concrete block wall. The wall was half finished.

"You have to come in on the level and leave on the square," Philip said in a cocky tone. Jim turned around with a squint in his eyes and a quizzical look on his face. He stared at the lanky lad and was about to say, "Who the hell are you?" when he recognized him.

"But did he leave on the square?" Jim replied.

This time Philip looked surprised.

"You've read Kipling?" Philip asked.

"That and most everything else," Jim said. "How's your brother?"

"He's still in the hospital with pneumonia, but he'll be okay."

"Are you working this summer?"

"No, not quite old enough. I missed it by a couple of months."

"Are you afraid of heights?"

"No, why?"

"I have a job for a sure-footed Indian," Jim said.

"Like what?"

"I need a 'rod buster' and someone to do odd jobs around here."

Philip looked around the job site and noticed the steel rods sticking out of the freshly pour concrete and he knew what Jim was referring too.

"I can do it."

"Can you start tomorrow?" Jim asked. "Today you need to help your mother clean up from the storm."

*****

Kate was out of business for over a week. It took her two days to clean the shop after the storm. She got rid of the melted ice cream and cleaned the coolers. Everything that was in the refrigerator and freezer was spoiled. She put a claim in to her insurance company, and after the deductible she received only sixty per cent of what she lost.

Steven recovered from pneumonia and returned to work slowly, putting in one day a week. Philip liked his job working for Jim. Isabelle loved real estate school, but was still somewhat cool to Kate. Everyone and everything was in a state of grace.

Kate started thinking about her future, trying to make plans. She knew she had about six months before the demolition of Shell Creek Bridge. If she could get through another season, that would be fine with her. She set her goals for the first of the year, which gave her time to look for another place to live.

*****

The door jingled open and the Professor stumbled into the shop. "Kate, are you in?"

Kate peeked around the corner. " Hey, Professor, how are you doing? Haven't seen you in a long time." "Would you like some coffee?"

"That would be perfect," as he slipped into one of the ice cream chairs.

Kate brought over two cups of coffee and sat down beside him wondering, why is he here? They both started talking at the same time. Kate jestered with her coffee cup, "you go first."

"Well I have been contemplating, about you. Do you have any idea, where you are going to live?"

"I have lost sleep over that question."

"I have a proposition. Do you know where kittle harbor is? Your boys fish in there all the time. Beyond the water edge lies a beautiful piece of land, high with access to the to the Gulf and to the Intra Coastal Waterway. If you like the looks of the property it would make a profitable investment for you. Have your son, Steve take you for a boat ride." A somewhat astonished Kate didn't know what to say. The professor patted Kate's hand." Think about the proposition, let it find roots in your mind, talk it over with your boys and let me know. I Like your sons and I would like your family to remain in the community."

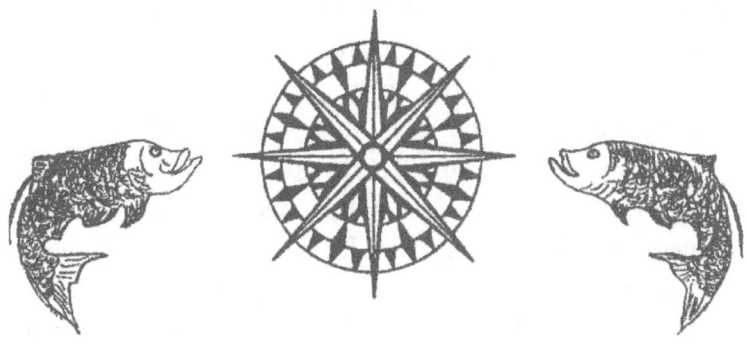

Whisky Corners

*K*ate was sitting at an ice cream table making lists of things she needed to do before the first of the year when Big Jim walked into the shop.

"What brings you here?" she asked.

"A date," he answered. "You ever been to Whisky Corners? I thought you would might like to view the mating rituals of the Florida Redneck"

"Are we going to view the rare Florida Redneck in full plumage?"

"It only occurs on Saturday night." Jim smiled.

"Only if we are talking about the authentic Florida Redneck and not some hybrid from Georgia?"

"Those from Georgia are called 'Imitation Crackers.' They are rather thin and flaky like any other cracker."

"Well, if you are going to escort me to the infamous watering hole to see the authentic rednecks in full plumage, how can I possibly refuse?"

"Good, I'll pick you up at eight o'clock Saturday night, we will walk, and it is only a short block."

"See you at eight, then." Kate said.

Jim turned and left without another word. Kate watched him ride away in his Jeep. Whisky Corners sits in the intersection of State Route 776 and Placida Road, in an old clap board building about seventy years old. It must have been there for years because the intersection goes around the building. Placida Road wraps around the north side of the parking lot, crosses Rt. 776, and changes its name to Pine Street Then it meanders a few hundred yards, turns into a shell road, and dead ends in a marshy landscape full of pine trees, hence its name. The marsh is full of alligators, snakes, scrub jays, water birds, quail, and a lots of other Florida natives. Some claim to have seen Florida panthers roaming around the marsh on Pine Street.

Going south on Placida Road there is an ice cream shop on the right and on the left is what's left of Bob's Bait House. Further down starts the new construction of Gasparilla Land Development, which goes to Route 771 and makes the turn east to El Jobean.

Saturday night came and Kate dressed in tight pair of

blue jeans, with a pink chopped T-shirt, a pair of gold-hooped earrings and a pair of sandals. When in Rome...she thought. Jim scratched on the side door. Kate answered the door. Jim eyed her up and down grabbed her hand and started to walk to Whisky Corners.

"Tell me." Jim asked. "What color is your hair, black or red?

"Both. If I am in the sun my hair looks red."

"Does the collar and cuffs match?" Jim looked at her with a side-glance. Kate matched his glance, shrugged her shoulders and kept on walking

As they were walking through the parking lot, Jim asked, "There will be a lot of red necks in heat, aren't you worried?"

"I'm with a great big hound dog," she replied. "I should be perfectly safe." Kate stepped in front of him and walked into Whisky Corners.

Whisky Corners was a bar with a reputation, the only bar with a drive-through window for your entire alcoholic needs. It was famous for its Saturday night fights, and its Friday night fights, and, Kate guessed, for its fights any night of the week. During the day the place was quiet and you might take a friend there for lunch.

But at night the place took on a whole new meaning. On Saturday and Friday nights a band usually played country music, once in a while one of the top twenty tunes is played. But for the most part it was county and Jimmy Buffet and the place rocked and rolled. Every redneck, fishermen, tourist, and anyone looking for excitement, went to Whisky Corners.

The long, curved bar made an L-shaped divider, splitting the large room into two separate areas. There were booths around the big room, leaving a dance floor in the center, and smaller part of the L had tables.

Jim found two bar stools in the middle of the L. The band was playing a county song and they were quite good. The bar soon became very crowded with standing room only. Kate noticed that most of the men wore jeans and polo shirts, baseball caps or a Texas ten-gallon. Everyone had cowboy boots. The women wore a variety of clothing from jeans to bikini tops with shorts, pants, Mu Mus, fancy dresses and even some formal evening clothes and sarongs tied at shoulders. Kate looked to check if Jim was wearing his expensive boots.

"I see you have your expensive boots on."

"What else?"

Jim did not sit on the barstool. Instead, he used it as a leaning post. His right foot rested on a rung of the stool while his left foot was squarely on the floor. He leaned into the bar with his right elbow resting on the bar. He looked very relaxed and comfortable. Jim drank with his right and he kept his left hand on his left leg. Kate noticed he did not drink very much. She figured him as a man who could drink and hold his liquor. He smoked slow and deliberately and sipped his drink.

A women who sat next to him was telling everyone at the bar how she murdered her husband and disposed of the body by putting him into the septic tank.

"He accused me of serving him shit for dinner," she said, slurring her words. "I fixed him. Now he is in shit with all he can eat, the bastard,"

Everyone laughed. What a hoot.

Unexpectedly, the women next to Kate chimed in with her story. "Honey you think that is bad, my old man tells me he doesn't want sex because it makes him too tired to work the next day."

"Hey lady, anytime you're horny you just call me. I am never too tired for a turn in the hay," some guy at the other end of the bar shouted back.

"There are three things that are important to a redneck: one, is his dawg, two, his gun and third, is his pick-up truck. Don't forget that." They bantered back and forth for while then settled down.

Kate sat with feet locked on the rungs of the barstool and both elbows on the bar. She was faking it, but she looked like she spent all her life in a bar. Oddly enough, she found that she liked the crazy people and weird atmosphere. Jim asked about Steven.

"He's still a little weak," Kate said, "but he's coming along fine. I just want him to rest a little while before going back to work full time."

They talked about the No Name Storm, the flooding, the damage, loss of her inventory, and the shop closing for a week. Jim told Kate that the road was flooded and it was not navigable enough for workers to enter the development.

"Don's negotiating with the county to raise the height of the road for access," he said. He also mentioned that Philip was proving to be a great help to him and that he would keep him working until school started.

"Is your son, Steve, and his friends still exploring the waters and islands in Charlotte Harbor?" he asked.

"He has not gone anywhere the last two weeks," Kate said. "I don't know about exploring, but I know they fish a lot. They've caught everything from pompano, flounder, grouper, snapper, redfish, and trout to sea bass, blowfish, sail cats, and mackerel. I've had to learn to cook blowfish and stingray. They have traps out for stone crabs, blue crabs, they have netted for shrimp and mullet, and they dig for clams and scallops. Why do you ask?"

"Oh I just thought I saw some kids around Catfish Lagoon a few week ago.

Kate shrugged her shoulders and sipped her drink.

"Have you ever gone for oysters?" Jim asked.

"No."

"Well, let me introduce you to oysters." Jim looked up into air like he was calculating, then took a drag on his cigarette.

"How about November, the waters will be cold and we need an R in the month for oyster."

"I will put that on my calendar."

Jim asked Kate to dance and they hit the floor for several tunes. For a big guy, Jim was a very smooth dancer. They went back to the bar and ordered more drinks.

"Have you decided what you will do when you are forced to close your store?" he asked. "Have you made any plans?"

"No, I've been thinking about doing different things but nothing definite," Kate said. "I have six months, at least to the first of the year."

"Have you ever thought about renting your boat dock?" Jim asked. "It would bring a nice income. It has a good location, your right on the bay and deep water to Stump Pass."

"No I haven't given it a thought. Roger was saying that the previous owner had let drug runners use the dock."

"Roger's right, he was making big bucks, too."

"Really? Wow, I can read it now, 'Mother of two caught in drug smuggling ring.' I don't think so. Anyway I hate drugs and the use of drugs, they make imbeciles out of intelligent people."

Suddenly something went flying over her head.

"What was that?"

"Beer bottle," Jim said.

Kate looked to see where the bottle landed. Jim's left arm came up as he struck a man in his throat with the blade of his left hand. The guy went down cold turkey, then Jim kicked something across the bar room floor with his left foot.

A fistfight broke out on the other side of the bar and mayhem set in. Beer bottles were being broken, punches were swung, and groans and moans could be heard. Kate did not know whether to duck or watch. The lady that just buried her husband in the septic tank left her bar stool and jumped on the back of one of the fighters, she whooped and yelled and pulled hair, he tried to rid himself or her but she hung on to save her life. Out of nowhere Dwayne appeared with cigar in mouth and pulled her off the man and told her to sit down and mind her own business. She called him a rat but she stayed put in the chair. Next Dwayne bellied up to a guy who was pushing everyone; men and boys alike, down and kicks them in the side. Dwayne moved in, belly first, pushed him down with his protruding belly and told him, "stay down or I'll stomp on you." His cigar never left his mouth but he sprayed tobacco juice all the over the reclining man.

Behind her, Kate heard the bartender as he spoke to the law.

"Hello, this is Whisky Corners," he said into the phone. "There's a fight goin' on, so you'd better get down here and settle things. But take your time, don't hurry, I have a few bets placed."

Jim took Kate's arm. "Let's get out of here before the law gets here."

He literally dragged Kate out the door.

"What was that all about? It happened so fast. Did you kill that young man?"

"No, but he will have a sore throat, It's Saturday night and there is always a fight. It is the red neck way of letting off steam."

They walked back to the Ice Cream Shop in silence as Andy Struhart, our new Deputy, drove into the parking lot.

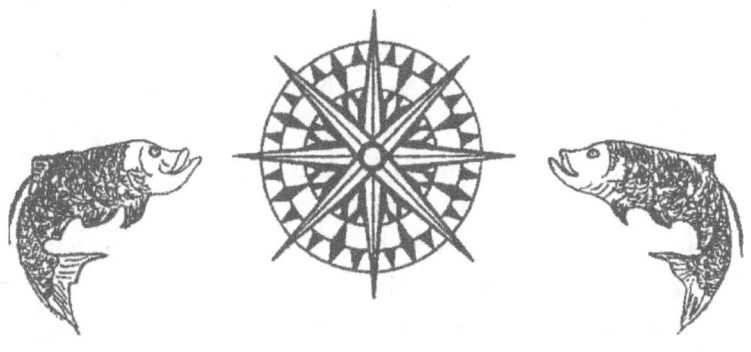

Oysters and Wine

Wednesday afternoon was sunny with a nice gentle sea breeze and cool dry air of sixty-five degrees. It was November, and the snowbirds had begun flocking south. The people who stay six months have already arrived, the next on tap are those who stay three months, they usually arrive after the holidays. March is the biggest month for tourists. But, as of early November, the roads are still unclogged and it was still possible to get a seat in a restaurant.

School had been in session for a couple of months and everyone was waiting for Thanksgiving.

Isabella received her real estate license, sold several houses, and made a lot of money. Don Buyers was ecstatic as his development took off. His project was forecast to do well. He was now starting to development the east side of the road; he planned to break ground in the spring. The Key was beautiful just as he predicted it would be. But Don realized he wasn't very popular. Even the locals who worked for him and took his money disliked him. They knew he was not only destroying their way of life, but also paying them to participate in the destruction.

However, the snowbirds loved his development. They raved about the amenities. The more the word got out the more they flocked to Buyers' paved-over paradise.

Jerry continued to pursue Isabelle who, despite her new money, clung to Buyers like a limpet.

The new deputy, Andy Struhart, has proven to be a good guy and a comfortable presence for a small town without crime. Andy has kept himself busy. He was usually called to break up fights on Saturday nights at Whisky Corners and he drives the drunks home. He has caught a few speeders but he has not given any tickets just warnings. When the one traffic light was out due to power outages, Andy was out there directing traffic. He was an asset after the No Name Storm.

True to his word, Don Buyers built the first firehouse. It was a great looking building, but there was no fire engine, or hook and ladder truck, or ambulance. The community was waiting for the county to furnish the fire truck and necessary equipment to fight a fire. They established a volunteer fire department but still they had no equipment,

Kate was in suspended animation. Steven would graduate in June and would be off to college in September. Philip would not be far behind. She was betwixt and between, so she tried not to think about the future.

November came and no surveyors or bulldozers had arrived. But she knows they are coming. The much-anticipated road between RT 775 and RT 776 is finished. Gossip has it that the bridges will be next.

The Crab Lady filed a lawsuit against Don Buyers. He said he owned the property that she lived on. She claimed squatter's right, and said her property is homesteaded.

*****

Jim just completed a big concrete pour on a condo; it was too early to quit for the day and too late to start anything else. He looked around, smelled the air and thought. "It's November and there is an R in this month. Might be a good time to go for oysters, we are at high tide. Why not?" He called Kate.

"The Ice Cream Shop."

"Would you like some oysters for your Thanksgiving stuffing?'

"Are you supplying the oysters?"

"No, but it is a beautiful afternoon for a boat ride and

digging for oysters. What do you say?"

"Now?"

"Why not, if not now, when?"

Kate thought a moment.

"You're right. Why not? Give five me minutes to get ready."

Exactly five minutes later Jim sauntered into the shop. Kate had just finished putting the 'GONE FISHING' sign on the door. She had changed into a loose pair of slacks and pulled out her yellow fishing boots and brought them with her.

"Ready?" Jim asked.

"Yes, I can't wait for some fresh sea air."

"Well then, let's go."

Jim drove south on Placida Road to where he had his boat docked on development property—a future building site, phase five, he explained.

"There are oyster beds in Bull Bay and some in Catfish," Jim said. "Let's go to Bull Bay first."

They took Jim's mullet boat, a very shallow draft boat. She remembered the last time she was in the boat; this time she was dressed more casual, no white suit today, just fishing boots, old slacks and a T-shirt. She knew the routine. Kate climbed in and sat in the bow on an upturned five-gallon bucket. She thought they would go down the newly finished Intercostal Waterway, but Jim went the backwaters. They wove in and out between mangrove islands. Here and there would be sticks or a broken branch as direction markers. If you did not know the markers you would be lost forever.

The Price of Crabs

After a half an hour or more they came into Charlotte Harbor and Jim pointed out the Gasparilla Pass and Cayo Costa. We're headed south, Kate thought. Jim slowed the boat and said.

"We're almost to Bull Bay, I want check out this island called Cayo Pelou."

"OK, what a beautiful day for exploring."

"Can you swim?"

Kate nodded

"You may want to carry your sandals." Jim anchored the boat off shore. Kate fastened her sandals together, wrapped them around her arm, and swam ashore. Jim was right behind her. Once they were ashore they put their sandals on and walked into the interior where it was dark and cool. The foliage was so thick the sunlight could not penetrate. Jim seemed to know where he was going. Kate just followed after him.

They walked awhile until they came across a bulldozer with a large blade.

"What the hell is that thing doing here?" Kate said. "This is an island right?"

Jim did not say anything. He just walked around and climbed up to see if someone left a key in the ignition. Satisfied, he climbed down, grunted, and continued to walk.

Kate pressed the issue. "How did that get here?"

"There's a boat dock on the back side of the island."

Kate noticed a swath that was cleared behind the dozer, large holes that look like dugout fox holes, and markings on the palm trees.

"Are those marking and holes from the same Spanish pirate? Just like ones that were on Mound Key? Or, are you building an exclusive gated community?

"No."

Jim's answer was a bit too fast for Kate. She gave him a look that said, "Really?"

"No" Jim said again. "The man that owns the island is doing some landscaping."

"Yah, a real botanical garden," Kate said

"Well, I've seen enough, let's go find some oysters." Jim started moving toward the water. They swam back to the boat. Kate looked at the Intercostal Waterway and back at Cayo Pelou. She noticed that the backside of this island could not be seen from the Waterway. Not only that, why did we swim ashore? This is a mullet boat; built for shallow water. There is a mystery here. Something is amiss Kate thought.

Jim swung around Bull Bay and pointed out the fish shacks that stood on stilts in the middle of Bull Bay. "These shacks are remnants of the old mullet fishing community. The fishermen lived on them during mullet season; they would hang their nets over the decking to mend. Those shacks could sleep four to eight men; they would tie their boats up alongside and fish day and night. At one time there were twenty-five shacks; now only seven were left. They have become tourist attractions."

"They are quite romantic." Kate said. Jim turned the boat around and headed toward Catfish Lagoon.

Mullet Fisherman Shacks - Bull Bay - 1986

Catfish Lagoon was a pretty area. It was very shallow in places and then got deep in spots. Jim pulled his motor up and they drifted over oyster beds. He was looking for the perfect bed.

"The best oyster beds should be under water," Jim explained. "They should always be covered with at least eight inches of water, even at low tide. If not the whole bed can become tainted."

Kate was thinking that one bed looked the same as the next when Jim found the perfect oyster bed. The bed was at least a foot under water. It was a very old bed and large.

"How do you know if this bed is an old one?"

Jim took a knife from his pocket and slipped over the side of the boat. He bent down and snapped an oyster off. When he came back up he showed it to her.

"Oysters are like trees," he explained, "they have rings that show age; each ring represents a year, this one has three rings. He took his shucking knife, opened the oyster and ate it right there. He licked his lips. "Delicious. "Put your boots on and hand me a bucket. Get in the water and let's get some oysters."

Soon both Kate and Jim had filled their buckets. They got back into the mullet boat and Jim showed Kate how to shuck oysters. She caught on fast. She started to throw a shell over board when Jim grabbed her arm.

"Don't do that."

"Why?"

"Because the star fish will smell that discarded shell. One star fish can destroy a oyster bed."

"I didn't know that." Kate said.

"They send out a message and in a short time every star fish, their aunts, uncles, grandchildren, mom and pop will be here and every oyster will be eaten. The natural enemy of the oysters, besides man, is the starfish."

Kate shucked an oyster and sucked the meat from the shell. It tasted salty and it was very warm, not like what she was used to in a restaurant where they are served them on a bed of ice and very cold. She was surprised they tasted just as good warm. She shucked another oyster and the juice started to run down her chin. She looked around for something to wipe her cheeck and chin but there was nothing. So she took the end of her T-shirt and wiped her chin. She noticed Jim watching her. He took in every movement. He sat in the seat behind the wheel smok,ing a cigarette and watched her every move especially when she exposed some flesh on her midriff as she wiped her chin with her T-shirt.

"What are you thinking?"

"Something about a woman slurping oysters," he said with a smile. Kate noticed his green eyes begin to water and she thought there is more to Jim then what meets the eye.

Jim reached into a small cooler and pulled out a bottle of Mateus, two wine glasses, cocktail sauce, and a small box of saltines. They ate and drank in silence for a while.

"I have not had Mateus in years," Kate said. "I forgot how much I like the wine."

"Me too, I was introduced to Mateus in Portugal."
"Three years ago."

"Where in Portugal?" Kate asked.

"Funchal" Jim answered.

"I've been there, years ago."

"Really?" Jim said, but the look on his face said, 'I don't believe you.

"Where did you stay?" Kate asked Jim, but he gave her an off-the-wall answer and Kate did not believe him either. But in essence they were both telling the truth.

They drank the bottle of wine and ate a dozen oysters each. The sun started to set beyond the horizon as Jim cleaned his boat. Jim started the boat and cruised at a slow speed.

"Do you mind if I make a stop to check on a friend?"
"No, not at all."

They did not go far when Jim pulled up beside a huge brand new boat dock. It had to measure about twelve feet wide and at least fifty feet long. The dock was so new you could still smell the creosote in the wood. Jim climbed out of the boat and Kate followed. She looked around and found no reason for a dock that size. There was a gravel road from the dock that went into the thick foliage. Kate felt a little strange. An eerie feeling came over her. There was a shack and Jim scratched on the door. Then he opened it and entered. Kate stood outside and looked inside. It was a one-room shack. It had a single bed against a wall, a table and two chairs in front of the window, and a makeshift kitchen with a generator. It had a hand pump for water. Jim looked around, opened a cabinet door, and looked into a pot.

"No one is here, let's go."

On the way back to the boat Kate asked Jim.

"Is this piece of land an island?"

No, it is adjacent to the salt flats."

Kate said in a half apologetic voice. "I haven't lived here long but, where are the salt flats? I just found out about the point recently."

"Don's development ends at the beginning of the salt flats. Route 776 makes a turn east to El Jobean and becomes RT 771. The salt flat begins just after the turn in the road. Ask your son, Steve, he knows where the salts flats are."

"So from here we could walk to the road."

"With difficulty," Jim said. "It would not be a simple walk. The path is swampy, there is a marsh and the path is not well marked."

Kate looked at the immense boat dock and her mind went around in cycles. She would ask Steven about this place when she got home.

The boat ride home was quiet and peaceful. She could not help but think there was always some mystery about Jim.

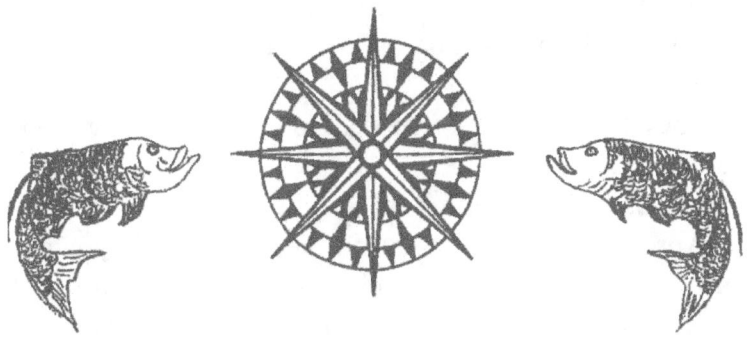

Black Night at Catfish

S teve turned off the motor and slid the boat into a cove on Catfish Creek. He let the boat drift with the tide; up the creek several yards, then he and Philip pulled it ashore and anchored it. They were both dressed in what they thought were commando outfits, blue jeans and dark long-sleeved shirts. They crouched and crept slowly through the blush.

When they caught sight of the large wooden pier they stopped and crawled behind two palmettos. The night was so dark that it was almost impossible to make out objects. It was the first night of a new moon and no shadows were cast by ambient light. Steven pointed toward the cabin, where a dim light shown through a window.

"Someone's there," whispered Philip. "What's supposed to happen here tonight?"

"One of the kids at school said his father told him something big was gonna happen tonight. So I thought we would check it out."

They heard the grass rustle. Both boys lay down on their stomach.

"Just a lizard," Philip said

Apropos to nothing, Steven asked, "What did you do with all those quarters you picked up a few weeks ago?"

"I'm saving my money to take a girl out on a date."

"Who?"

"It is a toss-up between Jim's daughter or Jerry's." Philip said.

"You're kidding I didn't know they had daughters."

"Well, Jim has two daughters. One is a year older than you; real pretty and she likes to fish. The other one is my age and she is cute too. I saw a picture of Jerry's daughter and she is a knockout. She is coming to Florida during Christmas."

"All I can say, is don't mess around because if Jim doesn't kill you Jerry will," Steven said.

"What do you think I am?"

"Shh, someone is coming." Steven pointed toward the dock.

Four mullet boats pulled up to the dock. They had no running lights and their motors were turned off. They slipped silently through the water. A man climbed out of each boat and made sure the boats were square with the dock. A second man climbed out. The men muttered in low voices. Philip and Steven could not hear what they said but they would catch a word here and there, something about trucks and meeting someone."

As they watched from their hiding place among the palmettos a man emerged from the cabin. He walked slowly to the dock, where he and the eight men who had landed discussed things in hushed voices. The man from the cabin appeared to be giving directions.

Suddenly a low rumble echoed from the brush. Two black paneled vans backed up to the dock. The sailors jumped into the mullet boats as the man from the cabin gave directions to the drivers of the vans. Walking backwards, he made gestures to the drivers as they expertly positioned the vans onto the dock. Doors opened.

"What's going on?" Steve asked.

"Shh, watch this," Philip whispered.

Four men climbed out of the boats and started to transfer square bales to the men on the dock, which they carried them into the waiting vans. The men in the boats were placing the bundles on the dock faster than men could put them in the van. The man from the cabin began to help.

"Hurry, hurry," urged one of the men.

"If we got one of those bales you wouldn't need money for college and I'd have enough money to date," Philip whispered.

"But Mom would kill us."

Suddenly, a hand grabbed each boy behind the neck. Calloused thumbs and fingers pressed on both sides of their necks, choking off their carotid arteries. Steven withered and Philip gasped.

"What are you doing here?" A deep, gravelly voice connected to the steely hands asked.

"A snipe hunt?" Philip croaked

"Try again."

"We were checking things out." Steven said.

"Can I date your daughter?" Philip croaked as he recognized the voice.

"If you survive the night," Jim answered with a chuckle. "Steve, where did you hide your boat? You have to get the hell out of here, and fast!"

"In the mangroves over there," Steve pointed.

"Here is what I want you to do," he whispered. "When I go over and talk to those men, I will scratch my head. When I do that you take off. Get in your boat and head up Catfish Creek till you find the cut in the mangroves where Coral Creek comes in. Then go up the creek 'til you go under the railroad trestle and head out to the harbor. Go back under the trestle again and head home through the Intercostal. Don't make a sound, do you understand?"

Steve nodded, his eyes big as nickels.

"Don't put your motor down 'til you are way out of ear shot."

The boys were scared stiff and crouched down so low that the wet moss was in their noses. They watched

Jim approach the men; he seemed to know them.

When Jim lifted his arm, stretched and scratched the back of his head, Philip and Steven crawled back into the mangroves, loosened the lines on the boat, and pushed off. They both got into the boat and let the tide carry them up stream. When the tide slowed they pulled themselves up stream by grabbing the mangroves. Once they were in Coral Creek, Steven started the motor. As Steven cranked the motor they could hear shouts, someone yelling, and what sounded like several gunshots. Steve put the motor in gear and they were out of harm's way in seconds. On the way home they kept looking over their shoulders, but they wasted no time.

They pulled up to the dock behind the ice cream shop and sat there discussing what they should tell Kate and if they should go to the authorities.

"Are you crazy?" Philip said. "Mom will kill us. And if we went to the law, I'll bet those men will kill us."

Philip said that when he saw Jim at work he would not mention a word unless Jim said something first.

"We'll tell Mom that we went fishing and could not find a fish. She'll believe that. At school I'll play dumb. One thing…"

"What?" Philip asked.

"I wouldn't ask Jim's daughter out for a while yet." Steven said.

The next day at school the gossip was that the law caught ten men in a drug smuggling ring. One guy was shot. The feds impounded four mullet boats and two panel vans holding $three million worth of cocaine and marijuana. The suspects were being held in the Charlotte County jail. But the whole story was still unclear.

Philip went to work after school and was told that Jim's father had a heart attack and would not be at work for a several days.

When Steve and Phil finally met later that day they exchanged stories.

"There were twelve men on that dock, the fishermen, two drivers, the man from the cabin, and Jim. The news said there were only ten. Don't you think that is strange?"

"Listen to this, when I went to work today, they said Jim called in and said his father was sick," Philip said. "How about that?"

"Something's fishy."

"How about the way Jim attacked us?" Philip said. "That was no average Joe Blow move; he could have killed us with that grip.

"Yeah, like, some kind of martial arts."

"You know, I'm going to ask his daughter out on a date and ask her if her father had any special training."

"I'd be careful there Philip. You would be entering dangerous waters. Think about that first."

"Maybe you're right, but someday I will ask that question."

"Let's just sit still and wait see what happens. Okay?"

"Okay."

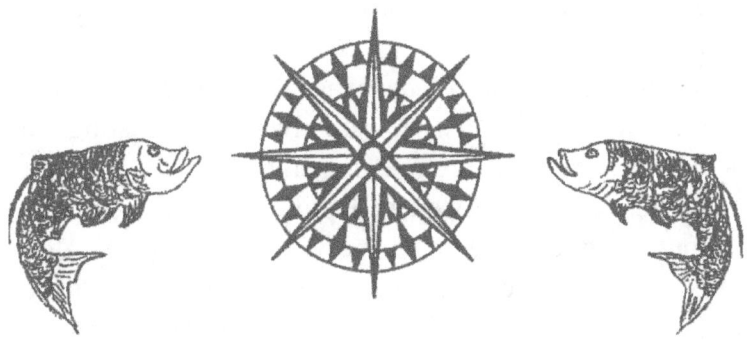

Indian Mound Saved For Posterity

*D*on Buyers was concerned about the progress of his development. He had Isabelle call Roger. When Roger walked into his office he asked, "How are things on the Key? Are we able to complete the work without Jim?"

"We should be fine," Roger said. "The first three holes of the golf course are done. That is all we planned on for now. The first stages of the condos are finished, next week we start on the second stage. We have the model for the villas done. You can open a sales office. The landscaping is finished for what we have built."

"Good. I want to take a ride over and check things out for myself. Let's take a boat and go over. I will meet you at the docks; give me five minutes."

Don straightened out his desk and left his office. He met Roger and they went over to the Key. Don had left the Key primarily to Jim's discretion. He was anxious to see the progress.

When they docked he was impressed with the landscaping; first impressions are always long lasting, he thought. He walked around the clubhouse. It was not quite finished but showed real promise. The first stage without landscaping looked marvelous to Don. He felt elated as he walked his project. In his mind's eye he could image the finished product. He wondered around the clubhouse. Roger kept silent as Don feasted on what he saw. Don roamed over to the first hole on the golf course and stopped dead in his tracks.

"What the fuck is that hill?" Don asked as he pointed in the direction of the hill.

"It's an Indian Mound." Roger said sheepishly.

"Roger, go get me the original plot plan and the surveyor original sheet with surveyor's marks. I'll wait here."

While Roger was gone, Don walked up to the mound. As he circled it he discovered a narrow path that wound around the mound. He started up the path. "That damn woman, will I ever get her out from under my skin?" he said out loud. As he walked higher it became evident a view was emerging. When he reached the top a red bark tree was in the center of the mound, a Gumbo-limbo tree. Under the tree was a small cement bench. He sat down and looked west into the Gulf of Mexico as far as one could see. I bet there is a beautiful sunset from here. He turned and faced east. He saw across the waterway and his land development on the other side and a view of the Crab Lady's property. From here it looked damn good. He was less angry now and could see the advantages of having an historic Indian Mound on his property that he preserved for posterity.

Roger rushed back with rolls of plans tucked under his arm. Don took them over to the clubhouse and unrolled them. Sure enough the stakes were moved; there was no Indian Mound mark on the surveyor plans. Instead there was supposed to be a golf cart path.

"Roger have you seen these plans?"

"No, I haven't. We went by the plans that Jim had."

"I see." Buyers rolled the plans up and told Roger to take him back to his office. I am going to fire the bastard he told himself.

Once back in his office he made a point of telling everyone. "If Jim calls, I want to talk to him."

Bocillia Pass - 1982

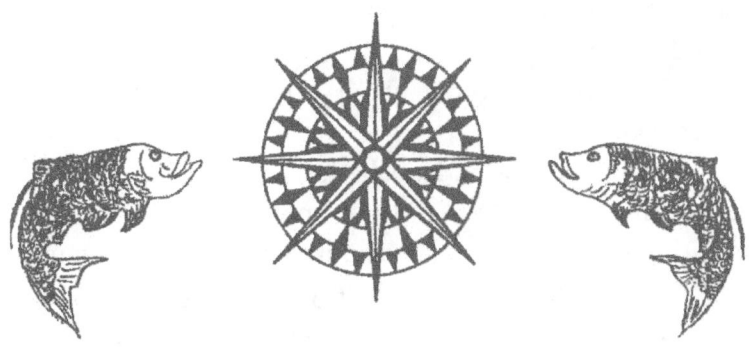

The Morning After The Raid

*H*arold entered the ice cream store with a dejected look on his face. "Did you know the surveyors started their survey today?" Harold asked Kate.

"How far are they?"

"They just got started."

Kate just nodded her head.

Steven came running into the door of the ice cream shop.

"I was on my way to school and I saw the surveyors, I thought I would come back home and tell you."

"So, I have been informed. It is okay. You can go back to school. Thanks honey I appreciate your concern."

Jerry grabbed his coffee cup and joined the guys. The five of them huddled and started talking in whispers. Kate noticed the change in atmosphere and became curious. She pretended to be cleaning the ice cream cooler and moved closer to listen.

"What do you know about this thing with Jim?" Roger asked.

"All I know is what Isabelle has told me," Jerry said. "According to her, Don did not know anything about a drug ring on his project. He said had he known he would have put a stop to it immediately. He fired Leroy and Ulee. One more thing, his operations manager has taken a leave of absence, family emergency. Don is keeping everything under wraps; he is afraid the news will ruin his development. Roger, you know Jim better than the rest of us."

"The operation's manager, wasn't his name Sellars or something like that or similar? Questioned Kate.

"Your right Kate,

"Well, there's a mystery somewhere in this mess," Roger said. "Jim came early for work before anybody. He was always checkin' things and snoopin' around. He made damn sure everything was completed on time and done perfectly on the square."

"'Enter on the level and leave on the square,' that is part of the Masonic Code, am I right?" Kate asked. They all turned and looked at her, surprised that she was listening. The fishermen shook their heads and shrugged their shoulders. None were Masons.

Jerry spoke up. "It goes something like that, I'm not sure."

"I do not believe Jim would do anything illegal. You might as well tell me about the mystery," Kate said and she pulled up a chair joined the huddle.

"I will tell what I know," Roger said. "It all seemed to start with the hiring of Leroy and Ulee. No one knew who hired them, but they did such good work no one followed through. The crazy thing is they were getting paid in drugs instead of cash. Who was paying them? Who hired them? Where did the operations manager go? Where is Jim? He could solve the problem?"

"Roger how did all this come about?" Kate asked.

"Have you heard of the Salt Flats?" Roger asks.

"Yes I have." Kate started to tell them about the oyster excursion with Jim but thought better.

"Someone tipped off the local authorities that a drug run was going to happen on a certain night on the Salt Flats." Continued Roger

"When the cops arrived at the Salt Flats they found four mullet boats anchored and tied to a boat dock with eight men, two in each boat. The boats had no registration numbers. There were two paneled vans that were packed to the brim with pallets of marijuana. They arrested all eight men impounded the four mullet boats and the two paneled vans. There are still questions to be answered and no one is talking. Andy, our deputy, was there but is not saying a word. That is all I know."

"Wow, this is a wake-up call." Kate said and left the table and stared getting ready for the lunch crowd.

The fishermen left. Jerry stayed behind. When they were gone Jerry asked. "How do you feel about the surveyors?"

"When I first heard the news this morning from the fishermen I was sick to my stomach," Kate said. "I knew this was coming and don't know why I feel so surprised. I have to make some quick decisions. I saw a house for sale not far from here that I liked. It has a couple of acres and a boat basin. I could fix it up and make it my own God's Little Acre. Oh! Did I tell you I rented this place with a five-year lease? Don recommended the location to the surveyors and they want occupancy the first of the year,"

"That gives you an income. You don't have to rent this for five years, why not stay open?"

"No, once I am gone, I am gone. I do not believe in going backwards or encores."

"You'll be missed."

"In six months everyone will find another place to gather and I will just be a memory. When I close, someone else will open an ice cream store. I was already approached by a person to purchase my equipment."

"Is there anything I can help with?"

"Jerry I have a confession to make, I am frightend, not because I have to start all over, I have done that before after Hank died and when I came here. But, of being alone; I like surrounding myself with people."

"Why didn't you have a relationship with Jim?"

"When we went to Whisky Corners on a date and a brawl started; he cut this guy down with a precise chop to the throat and at lighting speed. All I could see was a blur."

"Marital arts?" Jerry had a concerned look on his face.

"I don't know but it bothered me at that time and Jim knew it did. He brushed it off by saying the guy will have a sore throat."

"Hmmm, that makes me wonder. Have you heard from him?"

"Yes, I he left me a letter yesterday, but I threw it away, I was reluctant to open the letter."

"Why?"

"Because I didn't know how I would respond."

"You can't hide forever, sooner or later you will have to meet life, even relationships."

"Speaking of relationships. How are you Isabella getting along?"

Jerry shrugged his shoulder and leaned on the ice cream coolers.

"I don't know. She likes five star restaurants, expensive clothes, diamonds, and to be shown around on the arm of an ex-heavyweight champion. That is not me anymore. I can afford all those things but I am not there. Kate I am a recluse. I like fine dining like everyone else. I like a hot dog from a street vendor as long as it is good. Hundred dollar meals and clear cold Tanqueray martinis are not my goals. At one time, yes, I could drink a man under the table, but now I don't touch the stuff."

Kate looked at Jerry and saw the pain in his eyes; he was such a good persons and he is right about Isabelle.

"Don't give up on Isabelle. She's young, and that's what she's familiar with."

"It's not only that, we are not on the same page. I like opera, classic music, and jazz. She doesn't like any of that; I like to go to sports events, but if she can't dress up she won't go. I like staying home, she likes going out. She can't cook, clean house, or take care of anything. She has always had domestic help. I don't mind domestic help but I like my privacy."

"I am sorry Jerry, I thought you two were a perfect match. What are you going to do?"

"I'm going back to Brooklyn for a while, I have a gym I need to check on. I haven't been there for a few months. I thought I would spend Christmas with my daughter and maybe bring her back to Florida with me."

"What if Isabelle shows up in Brooklyn?"

"I would be delighted."

"When are you planning on leaving?"

"Next week. If I can be of any help to you or help with your move. I am here."

Kate came around the coolers and gave him a hug and he hugged her back, a big bear hug that surprised Kate.

"Will you continue to be my friend?"

"Of course." Jerry turned to leave. "Catch you later."

Kate felt depressed when Jerry left. She felt deserted. First Jim and now Jerry. But I knew Jim was going to leave. I saw it in his eyes when we were eating the oysters. I knew it then. Now Jerry. I hope Isabelle comes to her senses, maybe if I talked to her. This will be a lonely place if I stay, especially without the Ice Cream Shop. What I am going to do with the rest of my life?

The Price of Crabs

Just as Kate was feeling sorry for herself the Old Professor walked into the Ice Cream Shop.

"How are you," asked Kate. "I haven't seen you for a long time."

"How are your boys?"

"They're in Africa looking for the infamous Rhinoceros." The Professor laughed. "So you know about our conversation."

"There are no secrets in this family. They ask about the pheromones that are aphrodisiac."

"Kate that is what I like about you. Your wit."

"Thank you."

Kate I know you're in a state of flux, I came here to make you an offer. I have some land in Kettle Harbor. I am going to offer you an option to buy and build yourself a home there. I like your family and hate to see you leave."

"Thank you, I am honored. I would need to take a boat on and off the Island, is that correct?"

"Yes, but you and Steven have boats, and once you get used to the idea of living on an island it is quite nice. It may be a little inconvenient but you'll get used to the run back and forth to the mainland. Don't forget you have your privacy."

"Thank you again I will talk it over with the boys, you have given me another option, and you made me feel wanted. You have no idea how that offer makes my heart rejoice.

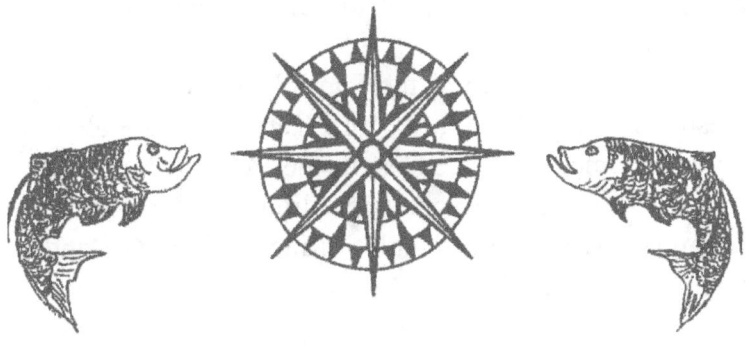

Consequences

Kate drove to the Gasparilla Condo Project Development to see Don.

He was outdoors directing and talking to a landscape architect about planting new trees when Don noticed Kate approaching.

"Hi Kate, to what do I owe the pleasure of your visit?"

"I came to thank you for sending the surveyors my way," she said. "They rented my property with a five-year lease. That lease makes life a lot easier; right now it is a game changer."

"Let's go inside and have a cup of coffee and we can talk."

"Good idea,"

Once inside Don offered Kate a chair. She looked around and saw how sparse the office was. "Where is everyone?"

"They're all down at the Sheriff's Office answering questions," Buyers said. "Look, Kate, you can always work for me. We need someone to help our new homeowners with their color selections and their interior design problems. There is a lot of money involved and a commission bonus."

'Thanks for the job offer," Kate said. "I'll give it some consideration."

Then Don got down to the real business of the meeting. "What do you think about this business with Jim and drug dealing?"

"I don't believe it for an instant that Jim would do anything illegal."

"Do you know where he is or where he went?"

"No."

"I would have thought that he would have told you."

"Why would you think that?"

"Because he's in love with you."

That statement shocked Kate. Her mind raced. She remembered the first time she met Jim. He was dirty, smelly, like he been out all night drinking, but he didn't drink. Had he been digging up pirate's treasure or a drug cache? Then she remembered the watery green eyes. No,

Jim is not a drug runner. But what was his interest in those holes, the bulldozer, and that over-sized boat dock? Was he using me as a decoy?

"What would make you think that he was in love with me?"

"Because he always spoke well of you," Byers said. He gave a thin smile. "And when I asked Jim to offer you a job, he told me you would rather sell ice cream at fifty cents a dip than work for me for any amount of money."

"He never offered me a job," Kate said. "But, he was probably right. At that time I would not work for you for any amount of money."

"I thought you two were an item."

"We went fishing, gathered oysters, and had a few drinks," she said. "Jim was always a perfect gentleman." There were times when we could have become intimate, Kate thought to herself, but it never happened, we never even kissed.

Don went for more coffee and refilled their cups. He sat down behind his desk and moved some papers.

"That puts a new light on things," he said. "Kate, why do you hate me?"

Right between the eyes. But Kate was ready. Like Jerry said, she could take a punch. Besides, things had changed.

"In the beginning I did. I hated what you stood for, progress, greed, conceit, ruthlessness without concern for other people," she said. "When you came into my shop that first time when you were looking for the Crab

Lady, you haggled about the price of crabs without any notion or knowledge how difficult is to catch crabs and the meager living they made. Then you fingered every greeting card in my display. I felt you were arrogant and self-absorbed."

She paused and took a deep breath. It felt good to vent. "But Don, I mostly hated you because you represented change—and not necessarily for the good. I loved my way of life, my customers and the old-timers with their stories, and the freedom to put the 'GONE FISHING' sign on the front door and just go fishing. Where in the world can you do that? This project is beautiful but it is has changed my life, the Crab Lady's, Jim's, Isabelle's, Jerry's and the lives of a whole lot of other people who have not come here yet. Just think of changes the county and state have made to accommodate this development."

Don had stopped fumbling with papers and was listening, pursing his lips as Kate talked.

"You're right, Kate, but in my heart I know it is for a better future; it will be a much more richer life style, better shops, better infrastructure," He leaned forward, as if closing a sale. "We talked about this before, Kate. The only tragic thing is the loss of your shop. At first I was trying to get back at you for that 'alligator mouth and canary ass' statement, but that revenge got lost somewhere and I don't have to think about that anymore."

"Well, you don't think about it because you got your revenge, now it is just a moot point," Kate said. "Frankly, I've gotten used to the idea of moving. To me it means a new adventure somewhere or here if I stay. You opened a whole new vista of life for me. And I thank you for that." She smiled. "I can't hate a man who does that for me."

All the way home she laughed to herself at the look on Don's face when their conversation had ended. When she pulled into the yard Steven called out to greet her.

"Hey Mom," Steven started to say something but when he looked at his mother's face, he stopped.

"You look like you swallowed a canary."

"I did. A canary and an alligator at the same time," she said. "By the way, I leased this property for five years, not bad, but now I have to make some decisions."

*****

Buyers needed a martini. He left the office and drove the golf cart to the new tiki bar and grill.

"Dave can you make me a Tanqueray martini with a lemon twist straight up"

"It will be right up Mr. Buyers," he said. "Beautiful day out there."

"Dave do you smoke?"

"Yes, but not in here."

"Could you give me two cigarettes I quit two years ago, and right now I need a cigarette and a martini." David fished two cigarettes out of his pack and placed them on the bar.

"Thanks, but do not ever give me another cigarette or you will get fired. This a one-time only deal, understand?"

"Got it, boss."

Don went out to the patio and waited for his drink. There was a man cleaning fish at the other end of the boat dock; a flock of pelicans circled, waiting for the cast off parts of the fish. He watched the man parcel out the head, tail, and fins and then cut up the remaining fish in small pieces. He tossed them in the water and the pelicans fought for the leftovers; Dave brought out Don's perfect Tanqueray martini, two cigarettes, and placed a Zippo lighter on the table, and left.

Don lit the cigarette and took a drag so deep that it hurt his lungs. "No wonder I quit," he said to the water. "The last time I had a smoke was on that cold night at Navy Pier two years ago, about the same time, end of November. Here I am again thinking about the same smart-mouth woman. That wench knows how to turn a screw. I fucked her good, I took her business, but she thanked me and told me it was a good thing." He shook his head. "Shit."

Buyers went back to his office and made a phone call to Harold Greenburg.

"How is our law suit against the Crab Lady doing?"

"She's going to fight you," his lawyer said. "She has nothing in writing but a good lawyer can cause delays; she has lived there a long time and has an investment,"

"Harold, end the suit. Offer some money, tell her the place will be the last parcel of the land that we develop and she can stay there for a reasonable amount of time. This way she will have time to get settled somewhere else. Also send down one of your minions to check out her boat dock, see what kind of condition it's in. If it is in reasonable condition offer to purchase the dock over and above the settlement. That should make things move along more smoothly.

"Don, you sure about this?"

"As sure as shooting," Buyers replied, then hung up the phone.

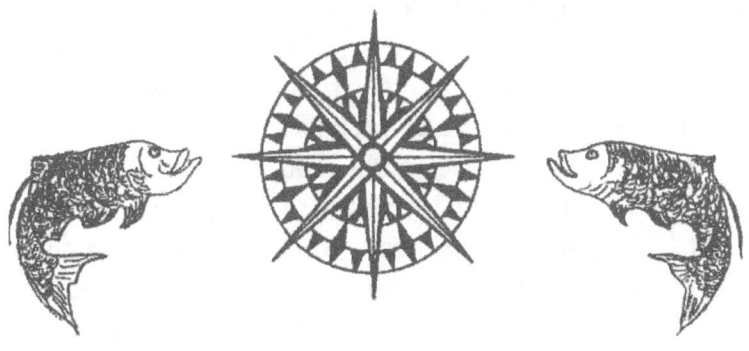

Reality and Conciliations

*A*fter Don had his martini and the two cigarettes he decided to drive down the road and check out the Crab Lady's place. It was more than two years since he visited her. It was déjà vu; everything was the same, as if time stood still. Their retarded son was playing under the tree just like before; he had a collection of toys. He pulled a small car through the sand making a noise like a motor. He had packed the sand together to make castles with roads or moats around them. He was totaly unaware that Don stood there watching him.

The Crab Lady came down the steps to greet Don. She was not as friendly as she was when they first met, but she was pleasant.

"Hello, Mr. Buyers, may I ask why you are here?"

"I thought it is time I stopped by. What is your first name, please? I really don't know."

"Rachael."

"How did a women of your stature ever come to live here and become a gatherer of crabs?"

"My brother, Michael, and I brought Tony here many years ago." She gestured toward Tony playing in the sand. "We came to get away from the authorities that wanted to keep Tony in school. They felt he would be better off with other children with the same disability. They tried to teach him rudimentary reading and spelling and some simple mathematics. But all that education only made him irritable, frustrated, and miserable."

Tony looked and grinned; he resembled a happy puppy.

"Although the authorities felt they were doing the right thing by trying to make him assimulate into society and teach him to read and write, he's not capable of reaching those goals," the Crab Lady said. "He is severely retarded. He is lovable. Although he may make some people uncomfortable, he is happy and content to play with his toys. That is the life God chose for him. So, we moved here to get away from the watchful eye of the authorities."

"I am sorry, I didn't know. It must be difficult for you and your brother. It also explains a lot of things."

"Would you like to come in for a cup of coffee?"

Buyers said yes. As they climbed the stairs and entered the shack, he noticed that nothing had changed except for the floral arrangement on the table. Instead of hibiscus flowers around the kerosene lamp there were colorful ixora cuttings. He gravitated to the bookshelves and studied the books again.

"Have you read all the Russian writers?"

"Yes, I used to be a literature professor at Boston University," Rachael said as she handed him a cup of coffee and motioned him to sit down at the small table. "

"Which Russian writer do you like the most?"

"Tolstoy is my favorite, especially Anna Karenina. I like how he describes the vulnerability of his characters and how superficial his characters can be when faced with the dictates of nineteen-century society. In reality love does not conquer all. What is your favorite writer?"

"Kafka," Don said. "I like everything he wrote."

"Existential realism," Rachael said.

"Exactly," Buyers said.

Rachael cocked her head. "Why?"

"Well, take Metamorphosis. He demeans himself from an exalted position; he justifies his position and then becomes critical of himself. I read him once for pleasure and the second time for meaning and understanding."

"The Chinese saying, 'You Americans read a hundred books, we Chinese read one book a hundred times.'

"The Chinese curse is, 'May you live in an interesting time." Don said.

The Crab Lady gave a thin smile.

As they discussed books, Don found that he was enjoying the conversation with this highly intelligent woman. Is this what they call a mental fuck or is this just mental intercourse between two people of like mind? He thought. I think I should get down to why I came here in the first place.

"Kate brought all the children's' books, crayons, and pencils she had in her shop for Tony. I am sorry her ice cream shop will close. It was a good place to go and mingle. We will miss her. Does she have any plans?"

"I'm not sure what her plans entail. But, I would like to know her better."

"You two were star-crossed. Many good relations begin out of adversity."

"Where is Michael now?" Don asked to change the subject.

"He's pulling crab traps. It is season so we are busy; he is getting blue crabs and stone crabs now."

"How long is season?"

"From October to the end of April, then we start pulling in the dollar crabs for tarpon season. You remember your friend bought six dozen."

"Yes, I remember, I came here and was jealous of your dwelling. It's simplistic and yet beautiful. I thought about the design for months when I went back to Chicago. My models have some of the same features; large overhangs, wrap-around decks, large windows, cross ventilation, efficient kitchen, and a large great room. Most of my ideas actually came from your place; I guess I owe you one.

The Crab Lady sipped her coffee, nodded her head, but said nothing.

"Were you planning on making this place your final home?"

"No, only until Tony becomes institutionalized or dies.

'My development project will not get this far south for another five to ten years. Would that time line work for you?"

"Possibly, but why would you even consider my future?"

"Because I am beginning to understand a few things."

Rachael stared back at Don. "Present me a plan that matches both our needs and I will consider the proposal."

Looking South on Manasota Key - 1988

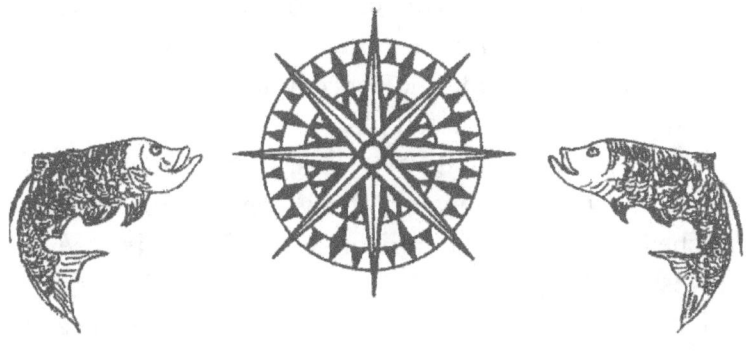

Sunset

*T*he sun was setting, casting a magenta glow over the sand and water. A zephyr from Mexico wrapped Kate in its arms and rustled the Australian pines. Kate was the sole human on the beach.

She noticed blue crabs crawling along the water's edge. The red glow of the setting sun made the crab's shell, gleam with a slivery blue sheen. I wonder how many people would appreciate the beauty, she thought, and how many would instead take the crab's home for dinner. Sandpipers played dodgems with the waves. A flock of pelicans glided on the wind and then dove for their evening meal. Seagulls made staccato squawks and fought one another for food. Kate spotted three porpoises out in the Gulf dancing, diving, and rolling in the water.

Kate closed her eyes and lay down in the sand. She listened to the sounds as the gentle breeze lulled her to sleep. Suddenly a cold wind crossed her body. She woke just as the sun fell into the water. "Maybe I will see the green flash," Kate said. She concentrated on the sun, but there was no green flash tonight.

The sky was a palette of colors; purple, orange, red, yellow, and magenta against fluffy cumulus clouds that stretched out against the horizon as the first stars rose in the western sky.

I once lived on an island between Shell Creek and Turtle Creek, joined by wooden bridges so low a person could sit on them and dangle their toes into the water, she thought, a place where children walked miles to school barefoot on unpaved shell roads or waited for neighbors' boats that would take them for their lessons.

People did not talk about hedge funds, dividends, and the stock market, but instead commented on tide changes, what fish was in season and market price for mullet, or the price of crabs.

The weather started to turn cold. Soon she was alone in the gloaming. How long will it take for the developers to destroy this solitude with high-rise condos, she thought. The universe gave us these beautiful places on earth free. Once they are discovered we put a price tag on beauty. Mother Earth did the creating, but we have to make an enterprise of paradise. Sell seats, parking spaces, and parcels of land, and leave nothing unscathed.

"Hi Lady."

"Jerry! I thought you were in Brooklyn?"

"I was."

"What brought you back?"

"I missed being here. This is home and I love my adopted family." Kate sat silently for a moment soaking in both his statement and the sunset. "What made you come to that conclusion?"

"Well, several things: First I am not needed. James can handle the business. He loves what he does, cash flow is plenty. I do all the books and bookkeeping, and I can fly up there once a month and check out things. I have no reason to stay. My daughter is happy. She will come down for Christmas but she wants to be with her friends for New Years,. Secondly I have nothing in common with anyone; they want to discuss boxing and reminisce. I don't want to rehash old glories."

"How did you know I was here?"

"Your son Steven." Jerry lit a cigarette, "do you mind if I smoke?" Kate shook her head, no. "Do you know the professor?"

"Yeah, I do."

"He comes by every morning for coffee, we have been talking about the development and the future. He started me thinking. I purchased an old building before I left for Brooklyn. Before I got involved in Boxing, while in high school, I loved welding in shop class. I considered it as a profession, but I got distracted. Don Buyers is looking for someone who could do welding."

"Don't tell me your considering a new career?"

"Not exactly. I am contemplating hiring a couple of young guys - I know a couple, and teach them; then open a welding shop in the new/old building I just bought. Don has thrown me a few jobs, like building his new boat docks, two pairs of wrought-iron gates, and some weather vanes. The professor wants to help, he is one smart old fart." Jerry laughed. "You know he dredged all the waterways when retired, even Shell creek and Turtle creek and made them navigable."

"Really."

"We also talked about getting service clubs down here to help people and to provide these young rednecks an opportunity for a college education. I have seen first hand what James has accomplished in Brooklyn. To be honest, Kate, I miss being here. I miss helping Steven with his truck, fishing, talking to you, talking to the old gent's that come in for coffee and I miss flirting with Isabelle."

" So, this is home?"

"I believe it is. I'll leave you now to your solitude, I apologize for interrupting." Jerry left Kate sitting on beach in the after glow.

Will this beach look the same in five years, ten years, or one hundred years? How long before it is consumed with commercialism? But Kate knew she was only a spectator. Once the door opened, the predators and the scalpers rushedd in to grab their share of the booty.

Kate sighed. I came here for a better life and I found that life with people I care about and respect.

She lifted herself up from the sand and stood there facing the Gulf. Out in the distance a storm was brewing. Silent lighting danced across the sky making an awesome light show. A few more stars appeared overhead in the now dark sky. Slowly Kate started to walk back.

Then she stopped.

"I can't leave here," she said to the sand and surf. "Why would I go back to a big city? I came here to discover a different lifestyle and I found that life in the beauty of the area and the people that share the land."

I cannot change the powers that be, but I can empower myself and create my own universe, a sanctuary, a place of peace and beauty.

Maybe then, she thought, I'll learn to appreciate the price of crabs.

Carolyn Siemon Schöner

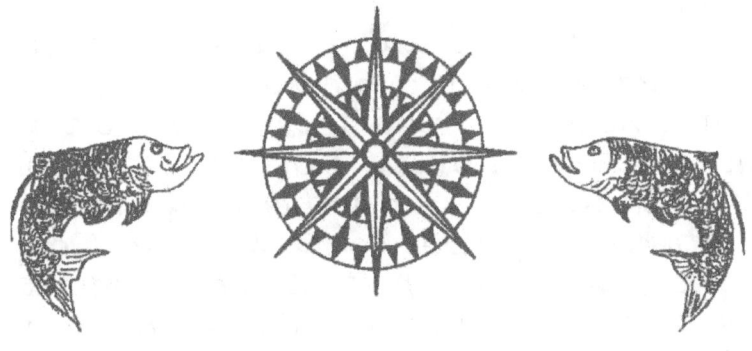

Epilogue

A lone man sat at a wooden table sipping a Turkish coffee and smoking a cigarette as he watched the sailboats on the Bosporus. A pen and some paper lay on the table in front of him. He gazed across the straits at Asia. His mind went back to a previous time. A time of excitement, hard work and special people. He wondered what would have happened if he had been able to remain in that little bit of paradise, even though the changes he had helped to make, made it less so. He wondered what changed had been made since his departure. What became of some of the people he knew? He regretted leaving so abruptly, but it was his job. Finally he began to write:

Kate,

I know you did not read my letter because of your provincial background, but I hope you read this. I was on a mission in Southwest Florida; I am in the Middle East on another assignment. In time things will be made clear. Don Buyers may be a pretentious arrogant bastard, but you can trust him. He is an honest man.

I hope you think about me once in a while as I often think of you. Are you still a Sweet Morsel?

Jim

The Insidious Predators

They come upon silver clouds,
Wearing diamonds in their ears,
They speak with slippery lucid tongues,
They come with insidious intent,
These predators.

Wearing a smile showing shiny white teeth,
They come.
Shrouded in self-righteousness,
With hideous sponges for feet,
They come.

They put strings on the poor, manipulate the weak,
So that their daily bread cost them their soul.
They step on the pious, and elevate the devious to the
dais.
These predators.

They feel their brother's wife, and
She dances to the tune of the golden coin.
They take what love is left and raise
Their clinched fists to the heavens and
Declare themselves gods.
These predators.

Thanks

James Abraham, my mentor
Jim Smith for all the help on the computer
Mathew Sweetnich, my grandson for the recent photo of
Stump Pass
Edith for her opinions
Steven and Philip for being who they are
Christine and Kelly for their support and encouragement
Ed Ellis for his advice
For all my friends and family for being there

I love you all

Cover photograph: Mathew Sweetnich
Author photograph: Jim Smith

A Conversation with Carolyn Siemon Schöner

What are your best memories of Englewood before development?

Having people over and barbecuing a wild boar or smoking mullet with all those characters from Shell Creek. I loved sucking oysters found in Catfish and Bull Bay. I liked Sunday afternoon canoeing to "killer bridge" and digging for clams off the sand bar that is no more, then going home, making clam chowder, drinking a cold beer and watching the football game.

How have things changed?

The Gulf of Mexico has been for centuries a wonderful source of food; and should be treated with loving care by the states and countries that surround it, instead of being exploited by oil companies and their methods of cleaning up oil spills. Our fish are polluted along with the water and contain a variety of bacteria. We are not good stewards of the earth. But it's still possible to change the direction of the maintenance of our planet.

But there must still be some remnant of that unspoiled life?

How about just walking a deserted beach without the presence of tall Condos and listening to sounds of birds, the whispers of Australian Pines and rhythmic sounds of the waves. Yes, you can still do that.

What do you want your readers to take away from this novel?

I hope they can join me vicariously in celebrating a past they may not have known. I hope to remind people that although we can kill what is most beautiful for the dollar, we also have within us the power to change things.

Have you seen any concrete examples of people winning the battle to clean up or preserve our natural bounty?

As a child, I played in the Cuyahoga River with my cousins; it was our sand box. I became interested in the environment when the Cuyahoga River caught fire in 1952. It was a common occurrence. In fact the Cuyahoga River had a history of fires. Solutions were always ignored or put on the back burner for a future project. My hometown became known as "the Mistake on the Lake." In 1969 the river caught fire again. Songs were written about the fire and public opinion brought about legislation that forced Cleveland to clean up its act. Cuyahoga Valley National Park was established in 2000.

This book is pretty funny to have such a powerful message.

You know, some of the best messages are lost because their proponents take themselves too seriously, and beat listeners over their heads with their argument. Although I'm opinionated, I can't see standing on a soapbox and lecturing until I was blue in the face. So I wrote a book, put some zany characters that lived in Shell Creek area, put words in their mouths and I spoke my truth. I added some history, mystery, and some tantalizing sexual images to get my message across without sounding preachy. Maybe the reader will feel enough awareness to make things happen.

www.ingramcontent.com/pod-product-compliance
Lightning Source LLC
Chambersburg PA
CBHW051335020726
47501CB00007B/2098